OTHER TITLES AUTHORED BY

SHEILA M. SULLIVAN

FICTION

Spectrum, Book 1 of the F.O.K. Series

Illumination, Book 2 of the F.O.K. Series

Shadows, Book 3 of the F.O.K. Series
(Coming out Winter of 2021)

YOUNG ADULT

I Want to Eat You Whole

NON-FICTION

The Accidental Writing Lab, A Collection of Ponder Points

PANDEMIC RABBITS

❖

AL,
You are Amazey!
Shelia M Sullivan

SHEILA M. SULLIVAN

Sullivan & Brown

ISBN: 978-0-9989648-7-4 paperback version

Editing Services by Kristen Tate at www.thebluegarret.com

Cover and Interior designs by Phillip Gessert at www.gessertbooks.com

Ebook conversions by Phillip Gessert

COVER PHOTOS

INTRODUCTION AND
DEDICATION

WHILE THIS STORY takes place with the characters from the F.O.K. series, it is not required to have read the first two books in order to understand what is going on in Pandemic Rabbits.

This story happened because my characters would not stop talking about COVID19. I was in the midst of working on Book 3 in the F.O.K. series when the world was thrown into a pandemic of horrific proportions. I had spent a few weeks in New York City with my Mom who was showing her Great Dane, Liz, at Westminster in February of 2020. It was amazing to be back in this city my Mom. She had introduced me to at the age of nine. As an adult I have had the pleasure of exploring the city many times. Now at fifty-one, having been in the city when COVID19 was taking hold I experienced a sadness rivaled only by the passing of my beloved, father, in 2016.

When I started writing Pandemic Rabbits it was April of 2020. The writing was dark, and my characters were not wanting to participate in the story. All they wanted to do was talk and try to understand what this all meant to them. Then one morning I heard Dana saying to get my butt out of bed and to get to the computer because the boys (Russell and Simon) were up to something. I listened.

When this story was finished, I realized that it touched upon the seriousness of COVID19 and there was something else, the humor of these wonderful brought hope. In their own way these characters showed me that it is okay to experience all the emotions that a world-wide pandemic brings, and this includes laughter. I do honor the seriousness of what we are all experiencing and bring with it a reminder that we need laughter and it is okay. I usually dedicate my books to one person, and, in this case, I dedicate this book to everyone. We are in this together and I hope this story brings a gentleness and peacefulness in a world that may feel as if it is careening out of control. Be safe and please take care of one another.

SHEILA M. SULLIVAN,
PLANET EARTH, WASHINGTON QUADRANT
OCTOBER, 2020.

TABLE OF
CONTENTS

1
FOOLS ARE WE

"I knew who I was when I woke up this morning, but I think I must have changed several times since then."

—ALICE, IN *ALICE IN WONDERLAND* BY LEWIS CARROLL

T HIS WAS HER happy place. Frances Olar Kavanagh walked to the far wall on the upper outdoor terrace of the San Francisco Museum of Modern Art and took in a deep breath. The terrace was rather packed with people this afternoon. The conversations mingled with the art to give Frances a reprieve from her loft and the past nine days of pure time lost to her painting. She leaned against the cool concrete wall and welcomed the overcast sky. A redhead coming out of the Northern California winter, she thought herself a ghost color with a tinge of blue. No direct sun today meant she would not go from translucent blue to lobster red in under twenty minutes. She could linger outside.

Frances loved watching people move around the sculptures on the terrace. It was where art and people could physically touch one another. No docents standing close to squelch the desire to reach out and touch, to experience the art.

It felt like a victory that she was even standing here. The boys had asked her to head to Petaluma to retrieve an antique sideboard. Old Frances would have said yes and put her work aside. No sooner had she said no to the boys, her phone buzzed with a another test from the Universe: instructions to be at Winter's condo to watch Autumn at 11:30 that morning as the nanny had called in sick. Was it a request or an order? Frances said no. That was it. No explanation. The word no. She smiled as she thought about how much she had changed over the past couple of years.

Frances took in another deep breath and as she exhaled, she sighed deeply. This was exactly what she needed after days of letting her creative energies flow. Once her energies to paint had arrived, she quickly built a dam of dirty dishes, laundry, and an unmade bed. It was her fear that the waters of creativity would keep on flowing into her and then out of the loft and down the street to another artist. She had to hold on to them as long as she could. To swim and dive deep into these amazing waves of creativity. Frances thought back to a time when she had scoffed at those creatives that claimed they could only create with a muse or energetic flow. She was not ready to share her deluge of inspiration that left her looking as if she was tumbled in a couple of giant waves and then spit out on a beach. She was swimming through this flood of creative inspiration with a new ability to hold her breath.

Nathan, her main creative mentor and the owner of galleries in San Francisco and now New York, was pushing her for the solo show in New York. It was less than two months away. He wanted it to open the same week as the gala at the Met. It was an ambitious timeline, and Frances had paralyzed herself in fear for longer than she cared to admit.

A family was stopped in the center of the terrace studying something. It wasn't a sculpture. Before she could investigate further, her phone vibrated with a series of messages.

She looked down to read from Dana:

They are closing the city. This shit got real...

Are you all right? I have not heard from any of you in two weeks.

They are closing the city.

The virus is here and they are closing the city.

The messages were addressed to her and the rest of the Buena Vista Irish Coffee Club. What was she talking about? Had Dana finally fallen off her rocker and entered into a place that was not embedded in reality? Frances knew that something was going on in China. But the virus wasn't in San Francisco. They had isolated the one person in Washington who had traveled in from China and tested positive. She glanced at the crowded museum and did not see anything that would suggest anything was closing, especially not a whole city Her world seemed to be functioning normally. What did Dana mean the city was closing? Could they shut down a city? Would they hang a *We Are Closed* sign on all the roads leading into San Francisco? Would a big red X be lit up on the runways at SFO? The airport never closed.

She sat down on a bench that gave her a good view of the rooftop terrace and, as Frances did when she is focused on other things, she bit her cheek as she responded. *Hey Dana, I don't think they can close the city.*

Frances, the Mayor of San Francisco is closing everything!!!! THIS IS REAL AND I KNOW YOU ALL THINK I AM OFF MY ROCKER. POPPYCOCK AND BISCUITS—CLICK THIS!

Frances clicked on the link and watched the press conference. Yup. "Shit." Her heart started to beat rapidly, and she felt claustrophobic. As she looked around, the crowd of people on the terrace morphed from art-lovers and tourists having fun into a mob of biohazards. The walls of the terrace and the sky closed in around her, making her vision tight. She couldn't see clearly. What the fuck was going on and where was Sam? She needed to call and talk with Sam.

She missed Sam more than she could verbalize. It was all of it she missed. Her touch, her soft voice, and the way her mouth would curve in a half smile when she was thinking of something devilish and fun to do when they were alone. Sam had postponed their rendezvous in February as her work schedule had her bouncing from New York to Seattle. Frances had said she understood. It was an attempt to be an adult in a real relationship. One built on honesty and trust. How she loved Sam and daydreamed about their future together was different than any relationship she had experienced in the past. A twinge pulled at her mind as she thought about Sam— she wanted more and did not exactly understand the cancelation. Sam had left her to create and paint and not pressure her to jump back into the world of what others called 'real work.' For Frances, joining a relationship with Sam had meant that she was finally at peace with herself.

Most of the time anyway. She realized that in thinking about Sam she had calmed down. Her world had turned into a beautiful place once she let herself enter that relationship.

Her phone vibrated her attention back into the present moment. It was Joshua.

Hey Frances, crazy world right now. We are still open here in Monterey; however, I think for the safety of my employees I will be shutting the restaurant. Theresa is still with me. Gotta go. If you need anything let me know.

What did he mean that Theresa was still with him? Theresa was the baby of the Kavanagh clan and the only one of the family still talking with her. However, they were not on the friendliest terms as each accused the other of sins that kept them separate. Frances hadn't heard from Theresa in over a month. Joshua was a special person to Frances and she hoped her sister had not screwed him over. She would have to find out what was going on, but right now she needed to figure out exactly what Dana's texts meant.

She flipped back to the text Dana had sent. No one had responded yet.

Hey Dana and our BVICC Crew—As Dana said, this shit just got serious. Round table at the Buena Vista Café at 3:00 p.m. If the world is ending, I want to go out with my chosen family drinking the best damn Irish coffee I can find! She reread her message after it populated in the blue bubble on her phone. No response.

She knew she was supposed to be sequestered in her loft working on her paintings for her solo show in New York. It was, after all, the reason she told the boys, Russell and Simon, she couldn't go to Petaluma. To say no to them was made a little easier when Frances rationally knew they really did not want her, they wanted her truck, Snow White. She'd gladly handed over the keys earlier that day, knowing they would return Snow White with a full tank of diesel and freshly washed and shined. They really were the best neighbors ever. Part of her had wanted to join them, poking around the antique shops and possibly stopping at a winery for a late lunch. But she had stayed strong and given a simple, strong no that had no room for questions or temptation. Russell and Simon had attempted to come in and see what she was painting, but she'd stopped them at the door and told them the unveiling would be worth the wait. And now she was wandering around her own form of church, the SFMOMA and a world of art, not at home painting.

Another message from Dana pinged on her phone. *Frances, the city is closing because the pandemic is here. People are dying. We are entering a modern day black plague and we are not knocking on heaven's door—if this is not stopped, we have entered hell. This is not a joke. Stop listening to show tunes and turn on your TV. I went to Target and a couple other places to get supplies. You need to get yourself to the store now. This is serious. No time for the round table. I am serious. This virus will kill you.*

Frustrated with the texting and wishing Dana would call, Frances took her earbuds out of her pocket. She was impressed that Dana, advanced senior in the group, had embraced the world of texting and FaceTime with her grandsons. Frances hit the call button on her phone.

Dana picked up on the first ring. "Hi, Frances. Don't be a knucklehead and get yourself to the store with a list of supplies. People are acting like the world is ending and toilet paper is going to protect them."

"Dana, back up a minute—or more like an hour. There can't be shortages of anything yet."

"Frances, do you not read a newspaper, listen to NPR, or turn on the local news? Sometimes I think my dog Shrimpie knows more than you about current events." Frances smiled and tried to let the dig roll off. Dana had adopted another beautiful dog from the no-kill shelter and named it after one of her favorite characters from *Downton Abbey*. Frances needed to follow up on the naming of Shrimpie. Later. She came back to the moment.

"No judgment. You know that I've been focused on getting my work done. I even postponed a trip to meet up with Samantha last weekend. I was going to fly up to Seattle. I miss her so much."

"Good thing you did because you probably couldn't get home."

"Dana, stop it. You're scaring me."

"This COVID-19 is something we all need to be scared about and now. We've lost so much time. The idiots at 1600 Pennsylvania are going to kill us all. Thank god we have some leaders locally that understand the grave situation we and the world are in, but then this is probably the wake-up needed. It is going to be painful and not easy. Hold on tight, Frances, this is going to get real—faster than anyone can imagine. What is coming out of Seattle and New York is beyond frightening."

Frances looked at her phone and Googled COVID-19 and San Francisco. The announcements were popping up. She listened through her earpiece as Dana explained how the virus worked on the system and what she had learned about how it was taking over in Europe and New York. There were cases in the Silicon Valley area, it was moving quickly in a nursing home in Seattle, and Northern Italy was in full disaster. Frances felt herself tumbling through an unknown reality.

"Oh my god, Dana, Sam's in Seattle and before that she was in New York. Shit. She's been working there since mid-February again as they are getting ready to open the latest store remodel for her client. I've got to go." Frances didn't wait for a response before hanging up and quickly punching the button for Sam's number. She stood as the phone rang for a third time. Most likely, Sam was in a meeting, and Frances found herself pacing around the people on the patio in the museum. This was crazy. "Hey, Sam. They're closing San Francisco over the COVID-19 virus. Not exactly sure what this means or how they close the city. Call me. Love you." She waited and moment and then added, "It's Frances."

She hung up and realized she sounded rather stupid. Of course, Sam would know it was her. In the time of smartphones, you pretty much knew who was calling you. Both a convenience and detriment, it took all the surprise out of a phone call. She took a long glance around her at the groups of people still casually enjoying the art in the museum and wondered if they knew the world—right here, right now—had changed forever. But was it going to change? She wondered if it really was as dire as they were forecasting.

The urgency in Dana's voice told her that her friend, the one who understood the impact of viruses more than the rest of the Irish Coffee Club, was borderline frantic.

Was it her age? She was reaching seventy-eight or was she eighty? It was hard to know because she basically never aged. Her garden, yoga, and the life of always learning was keeping her protected from the ravages of time. Dana often said the few gray hairs mixed into the blond were put there by specific teenagers she taught. When she graduated from teaching the gray hair stopped encroaching. Had Dana discovered the fountain of youth? She did claim there was a magic lemon tree in her back yard and was often plying the leaves and lemons as the elixir to cure almost anything.

Dana was always the voice of reason. Even if Frances did not want to follow her direction, in the end it usually was the right course of action. Was Dana right? Of course she was right, and that made Frances's body run cold and shiver. What did one do when facing a pandemic of unknown proportions? She took a deep breath and held the air as a prisoner in her lungs. She started to count in her mind, slowly at first and then faster. *Breathe*, her brain was screaming at her. Frances looked down at her watch. How long had it been since she took that long inhale? Was it two minutes? Five? Her face was flushed. What was she doing? Finally, she opened her mouth and let the air come rushing into her mouth, her throat, her lungs, eating the oxygen as if she had been starved of it.

Then she realized holding her breath had been an instinctual reaction to fight off panic. She did it a second time. This time she watched the second hand on her watch. As the numbers climbed to twenty-one, twenty-seven, her heart was pounding she clamped her nose shut with her fingers. Hang on, she told herself. Hold it. Hold it. And, bam, she let go of her nose and the air rushed in effortlessly. A slight feeling of calm was starting to descend on her. This breathing was not entirely unknown to her. A few years ago, when she was freshly mired in trauma and divorce, a therapist had taught her some breathing exercises and told her if they didn't work, she would prescribe some tranquilizers. When Frances asked for one strong enough to work on a horse, the therapist said she would most likely want to commit her. Frances learned the breathing exercises and never went back.

Frances turned back to her phone and stopped holding her breath. While it would have been understandably justified to drop everything and rush out to stock up on whatever it is one stocks up on when the unknown end of the world is quite possibly coming, she knew she needed to hang on to something that would sustain her and that was to get together with those people she loved. Sam was in Seattle and that caused physical pain in the center of her chest. Her love ran deeper than she often shared with anyone. "Fuck this shit. If the end of the world is not enough of a reason, then really there is nothing that would warrant calling a round table."

Frances and her closest friends had been meeting for several years on Saturday mornings at the Buena Vista Café for their famed Irish coffees. She was going to hang on to the Buena Vista Café round table. To double check, even though she had sent the request to the group already, she dialed the number and confirmed they were still open.

Would she have time to stop and get an Irish coffee at the Buena Vista with someone, anyone, from the club? Frances clicked into her Buena Vista Irish Coffee club group text and sent out the request again.

Round table at the Buena Vista Café—Not every day we are ordered to stay at home, and they close the whole city. I think we can make it before the city is closed down today.

Frances thought about it for a moment and added, *I don't want anyone to get in trouble. Do you think we would get in trouble?*

In one instant, her world had changed from one she felt certain she knew. A world where she procrastinated doing exercise, cleaning her bathroom beyond wiping down the sink, and worrying about birthing her paintings out to the world. Frances turned back to the people around her and it almost appeared that they were all moving in slow motion—as if her brain had slipped into time lapse as she attempted to comprehend exactly what she had heard from Dana and then read on her news feed.

Her phone vibrated with a response from Winter. *Frances, who is going to yell at you for going to the Buena Vista? You have some serious guilt issues to work through. Man, those Catholics know how to create doubt.*

Frances thought about it and decided she did need to recalibrate her brain toward authority. After all, it was the mayor of San Francisco who had issued the order. Could she do that and was it for real, or had some teenage hacker upset over losing in some video game decided to take it out on the Bay Area?

She turned toward the sounds of laughter and tilted her head. Had she really just seen a large white rabbit with a red jeweled collar hop around the LOVE sculpture on the patio at the San Francisco Museum of Modern Art? Had she been at the sculpture garden of the de Young in Golden Gate Park, it would not have surprised her; here, on the roof of the SFMOMA, a rabbit would

be strange although it possibly could be a new art instal-
lation. She shut her eyes and shook her head. No. That
could not have been a rabbit. She opened one eye and
looked to see if the rabbit was there. No one else appeared
to have noticed the rabbit.

To make sure that she did not see a giant rabbit on the
roof of the SFMOMA she took a couple steps closer to
a cluster of people posing for a group selfie. Behind them
she could now see a family gathered in the center of the
terrace and giggled as she realized it was a toddler wearing a fuzzy rabbit hat and a furry backpack. However,
that two-legged toddler rabbit was not wearing a collar.
Frances looked around the terrace and did not see what
she thought she had earlier. She felt her heart race a little and looked around to see if any other unusual things
popped out. This was all part of her psychosis over taking
a day off to play alone in the city. As she turned to walk
toward the door and exit, the white bunny with the jeweled collar and blue swatch of cloth that could have been
a halter top hopped from the LOVE sculpture to the wall
of shrubbery. Frances blinked hard. No one else seemed
to have noticed this bunny. Conversations did not break
or go silent. People were still focused on their phones
and looking at their little screens. Had holding her breath
caused her to slip into an alternate reality? Was she hallucinating a bunny? She looked back at the family with the
child dressed in the bunny hat. They were still standing
and laughing in a group. Back to the wall of shrubbery. A
large, twitchy-nosed rabbit stared back at her. His dark,
liquid brown eyes focused on her, ears standing straight
up and turning slightly.

She stepped closer toward the shrub wall. With her

hand open and outstretched as a message to the bunny that she was not going to hurt it, Frances crouched down and started to crab-walk toward the bunny. It was not lost on Frances that she did receive a couple of sideways glances and some finger pointing.

"Ma'am, do you need some help?" A young woman wearing a blue blazer, white shirt, and black tie asked. Frances closed her eyes and smiled slightly. She had caught the attention of a museum docent, who had her hand on a two-way radio. "Shhh," Frances whispered, "be very, very quiet. I'm hunting a wabbit." She tried not to laugh at her own joke.

"Um. You know I think it's illegal to hunt in the museum," the docent said seriously and muttered something into her two-way radio.

"I'm trying to coax that bunny. I think its lost."

"What bunny?" she said. "Repeat, I need some help on the terrace," she tried to whisper into her radio. "I don't think you can hunt imaginary things in the museum either. Is there someone I can call for you?"

Frances stood up straight, ready to point out that she was not crazy, and realized that is most likely what a crazed person would do. She tried not to laugh as she realized she was several inches taller than the young woman docent. She could pick the small woman up and put her in her pocket, she was that tiny. There was something that she found rather comical about this whole thing. Frances realized that she was now more interesting to the folks on the roof than the art as a crowd was starting to form around her and the docent.

"Is this a modern performance art piece?" Frances heard a bodyless voice from the crowd ask.

"Folks everything is fine. Please—"

"Doesn't anybody else see the bunny?" Frances asked and pointed toward the shrub wall where she had last seen the bunny. And, of course, the rabbit was gone. "Did anyone lose a rabbit that had a jeweled collar and blue shirt?" she asked a little louder.

A couple people smirked at Frances as they walked away. She turned back to the docent. "I'm fine. I'm telling you that there was a rabbit. A white bunny hopping around up here."

"I will have someone check it out."

"You have video cameras—have your control tower look at the footage. There is a rabbit loose in the museum."

"Calm down ma'am—"

"I'm not a ma'am—"

"Sorry. Do you prefer 'they'?"

"What? No. I'm not old enough to be a ma'am. I'm mean we are practically the same age."

"There's no way you're twenty-three."

"Ouch. I'm telling you there was a rabbit. I'm not crazy and I am headed out now. If you haven't heard—San Francisco has been shut down due to a killer respiratory disease."

Frances walked away from the docent and through the glass doors into a room filled with small wire sculptures by Alexander Calder. What was that about? She had seen a rabbit. Frances looked back to the terrace and the people. When she turned around, she saw a flash of white along the far wall.

Frances bit the tip of her tongue. She quickly walked across the room to get a better view of the wall. There it was again. The bunny had made it inside. As she stood perfectly still, she realized that had she said yes to any of the other invitations for her time she would not be going crazy stalking a rabbit in the museum of modern art. How could she share this fantastical story with her Buena Vista crew? The same group of people she had turned down under the guise that she was too busy working on her latest paintings.

As she inched closer to the bunny—now with both her hands outstretched, much the way she had seen people attempt to herd small toddlers—Frances's mind jumped to the absurdity of this moment. That rabbit was real. New Frances had learned how to say no to invitations, and she did not have to justify her field trip to the museum. Her largest no that she kept stopping to ponder was telling Sam she was not going to travel up to Seattle. Would Sam think that she really did not miss her? Why did that bother her so much? Frances realized it was because of the content of the paintings she had been working on, and she knew the doubt was creeping around the edges of this relationship. It was testing the doors and windows to see if there was a way to get in and obliterate it. Sam's long absence was starting to give more substance to the shadow of doubt.

Her normal paranoia about her work was not focused on the content, but on how others judged what she did. It made it easier for them to manipulate her into what they wanted, like using Snow White. A couple times she heard people respond with a not quite whispered "you're not really working" or "you can take the time." What she had come to understand was that her creative work was more important than anything she had done before. And that creative flow was not like reading a balance sheet or writing a financial summary. If she stopped in the middle of a creative burst, it sometimes was gone for good.

But had she turned into her own version of a prima donna? She did have an upcoming solo art show in New York, and every time she heard from Nathan the number of new paintings he wanted went up. Now it was at twenty-five, a number she felt tortured to complete in less than a year. Why this number? Other solo shows were said to be a success when the artist produced eight works. Maybe it was due to the size of the space?

Frances continued to crab-walk, herding the bunny closer to a bench and a pony wall that offered a view down into another level. A few more people came through the glass doors from the terrace. No one seemed to stop or notice that a woman was attempting to capture a bunny. When Frances was only a foot away from the bunny, a group came through the door, and the bunny dashed through Frances's legs and back out to the terrace.

Frances stood up and quickly followed the bunny outside. She could understand why the bunny would be attracted a wall of plants. Some were at nibbling height for the bunny. The plant wall formed an odd backdrop to the suffocating frozen snowman in box. This particular piece of art, by the Swiss duo Peter Fischli and David Weiss, always made her gasp for air. Effective art, she thought to herself. It elicited a response going to the most basic need, the need to breath. She *knew* the freezer snowman was not alive, but at some level her brain must have felt that he was—otherwise why would she always feel as if she was gasping for air when she looked at him? He was forever staring out through the glass door of his freezer casket. The green wall behind him, the sky above him, and the fixed expression on his frosty face mixed with the news swirling in her head made her feel both alive and a moment away from fainting.

"Beatrix. Oh my god, Beatrix, I thought I had lost you," a woman on a purple motorized scooter exclaimed as she motored past Frances and the suffocating snowman in a box. "Beatrix, you know you're not supposed to wander off on your own."

The bunny jumped up onto the foot platform and nestled between the woman's feet, which were clad in fuzzy slippers. Frances cautiously approached. Was the woman in the purple scooter real? "Is that your rabbit?" Frances asked.

"She's not a rabbit, she's my emotional support."

"A bunny?"

"She's a white Flemish giant and not a bunny."

Frances took a deep breath and started to back up slowly. She knew she wasn't crazy or hallucinating, but this woman with the white Flemish giant named Beatrix might be on that spectrum of questionable mental stability.

"Watch out, crazy lady," the woman on the scooter said. Frances turned quickly as a little rabbit toddler ran between her and the snowman, being chased by a larger child wearing a *Rogue One Star Wars* shirt and what looked like an Ewok strapped to his back. With one last look at the odd snowman and the kids running around him, Frances retreated into the darkened museum. The world was having a laugh at her expense now. She had responded to being called *crazy lady* by a woman who had an emotional support bunny. Her phone twitched, letting her know someone had responded—or maybe it was God calling to tell her she and the rest of the human race are fucked.

WTF! If the world is ending, I'll sing to the end with ya. See you at the BV, Winter texted.

Frances typed another message to the rest of the group. *Round table request number three. No questions. Did you not see the SF Mayor's order that we stay at home? This could be the end of the world, or at least society as we know it.* As she finished typing, she realized she needed to call Dana back and apologize for hanging up on her. She pressed her earbud and told Siri to dial Dana's home number. After the fourth ring, Frances hung up, realizing Dana was probably not going to pick up.

A text from Russell appeared on the screen. *Can't meet up as we are now on an extended trip to Gilroy. This is some crazy ass shit. Chat tonight when we get back. Snow White is sitting pretty back in her spot. Keys are on your counter. Toodles.* Why did he always end his text messages with a thumbs-up emoji? Did he not understand that meant a yes in her world? Frances smiled as she recalled the education Russell had given her on emoji and dating etiquette. He could not stop laughing as he told her she did not need to worry about the eggplant emoji—a joke she still did not understand. Now she didn't have to worry about that because she had found love with Sam, and their texting was special.

Well, Winter and I might be the only ones headed for an Irish coffee, she told herself as she worked her way toward the inner recesses of the museum. "Maybe I need to have a couple shots of whiskey, hold the coffee," Frances said aloud to herself. The rabbit toddler ran through the doors, squealing in delight and followed by two adults, most likely his parents, given they were all sporting very similar shades of white-blonde hair. Distracted by the joy in the toddler bunny, Frances decided to follow the group as they wandered through the museum on her way out.

As she trailed the group and glanced at the art, she realized that the free-play date she'd created for herself was not without focus. She often came here for the energy of inspiration. Was it the art? Or the people viewing the art that brought the sparks that would populate her creative energies?

Earlier, she'd wandered around the top terrace of the museum and had found herself drawn, as always, to Robert Indiana's four red letters forming the LOVE sculpture. She loved to watch people interact so personally with the letters as they took selfies with the sculpture. This morning, she'd watched a family as they placed one child in the cradle of the *L* and another poking out between the *V* and the *E*. She assumed the bearded man who climbed to stand over the baby propped in the arm of the *L* was the father. A woman with long auburn hair matching the crazy curly dark hair of the two small children framed the picture with her phone and counted down. "Three, two, Ollie and Lolo," she had yelled and the children snapped their faces toward her voice and giggled.

Frances smiled herself as she recalled the warmth of the smile on the woman's face when she had asked if she could help. Frances played through the scene again as she stood in front of a painting she had not noticed before.

The colors of blue, orange, and green made her think of something inspired by a Denny's interior.

"Do you want me to take your picture with your family?" Frances had asked.

"That's so sweet. Love it," she'd said and handed Frances her phone. "Ronnie, stay right where you are, she's going to take our family photo." Frances was struck by the ease of the woman as she ran over and placed herself at the base of the *V* and draped one arm around the toddler and reached the other toward the baby blob in the *L*. Frances had framed the picture and took a couple steps forward to focus on the faces. "Here we go. Three, two, candy," Frances yelled. That got the attention of the larger of the two small people. "I'll take a few more," Frances said and snapped a series of photos before handing the phone back. She heard the older one asking for candy as she walked over to look at another sculpture.

Frances was brought back to the present by the squeals of the giant toddler rabbit, who was now running a figure-eight pattern around his two parents. How was it possible to have that much energy? An image appeared in Frances's mind and she pulled out her small sketchbook that was always somewhere on her. She quickly drew out the image she saw and wondered if it would fit in the next painting she was working out in her mind. Despite the strange, unsettling news that exploded into her afternoon, she realized that she was actually relaxed and peaceful. It was a great afternoon to be procrastinating in the city. She loved the fact that the cloudy skies had given her the unofficial push to procrastinate and get out of her art studio. She filled her lungs and said out loud, "I love the smell of art."

"What exactly is the smell of art?" a woman standing next to Frances asked. Never one to miss an opportunity, Frances smiled. "It is this. In San Francisco it has a hint of saltwater, sourdough, and spice."

"I like that. The smell of art," the woman said and wandered off into the next room.

Frances realized that she needed to speed her exit up to get to the Buena Vista. Her mind fragmented and scattered, jumping back to her work at home. The paintings for her solo show were well into the final stages. Once she had found her muse, she had been off and painting one after another in record speed. It felt odd to be so peaceful at the moment. Maybe it had to do with her own blossoming love for Samantha.

But...did that make sense? Frances bit into her thumb as the woman in the paintings, the muse she had welcomed in, appeared in her mind's eye. A woman who wasn't Sam. How could she be professing her love to Sam but inspired so passionately by another?

"There goes my peace," Frances said and double-timed her steps. It was still a walk but one that might have others wondering if she was in search of a bathroom and close to losing it.

She was losing it, in fact—her heart was calling out to her. How could those paintings filled with sexual passion not be of Sam?

Picking up her phone to see if she had missed a text or call from Sam, she accidentally hit the photo app and her latest images, of the red letters captured in metal and paint on the terrace of SFMOMA, appeared on the screen. In that instant, she realized that she was craving the woman she painted in a way she was not thinking about her current love. Shit. This qualified as one heck of the wreck of the Hesperus, as Dana would say.

Her phone rang, taking her out of her swirl of crazy.

"Hey, Frances? Why the roundtable?" Dana asked.

"I was just thinking about you again. Sorry I hung up on you."

"Frances, you told me you had to go. No worries. You need to relax."

An audible sigh escaped Frances's lips. "Relax? You're the one that got me so amped up. I figured we don't know what is going to happen and why not close this day out with something that makes us all feel better. I wanted to get everyone together to plan too."

"I could catch a ferry and be over. I don't want to get into traffic. But what if they stop the ferry boats? I would be stuck."

"I promise I will get you home."

"I'll be there as soon as I can. How's the painting? You've been sequestering yourself for the past several weeks. You might be the one to get through this better than any of us," Dana said. "And you are going to take me home anyway—I want to stop at Costco, and you know we don't have one in San Quentin Village."

"The paintings are really starting to come together."

"Frances, are you pulling my leg? Dime to donuts you are further along in your brain than the reality of tangible work."

"Dana. I'll see you at the Buena Vista. Do you think it'll be busy?"

"No clue—guess we'll find out."

Frances took a long slow look around her at the people and the art. She decided to take the long way down and crossed the floor to the staircase. As she passed groups of people staring at their phones, she caught snatches of conversations as people discussed the stay-at-home order. One group was talking about zombies, but mostly people seemed confused.

She had made it to the wide staircase that led to the main lobby but stopped with her right foot hovering in mid-air over the first step down. She gripped the large rail and looked up into the white cylinder that was topped by a round skylight illuminating the lobby. It was dark. The gray skies appeared almost black—or was it the mood that had descended on the whole area? This was new territory and maybe those that read and watched all those dystopian stories were going to be right. Frances held onto the moment, wanting to stop time. It appeared to her that someone had turned the sunlight out. Would the light ever come back?

When she reached the floor of the main lobby entrance, Frances turned a complete circle, taking in the scene of her own special spiritual place—the house built with creative passions. When would she be able to return to her happy place? She remembered kissing Sam at the top of the stairs. It was one of her first public displays of affection, at an event that Sam had planned for a client that created some "googey gaggey," as Dana named it, that had something to do with art. The kiss had shocked them both and Sam had pulled Frances into her with some excitement. Sam had been wearing a tuxedo dress that had redefined beauty for Frances and made her lose herself in the gorgeousness of her woman.

Frances took in a deep breath and closed her eyes. She wanted to record this to her long-term memory. With her eyes closed she noticed the museum had a distinct smell, another layer to the normal smell of art for her. An aroma that was a mix of fresh paint, coffee, and rather stodgy body odor. She pried one eye open and searched for the offending smell threatening her memory. Her gaze settled on a person—a man or a woman? it was difficult to tell—wearing multiple layers of clothing and carrying two overstuffed reusable shopping bags. Frances felt a twinge of judgmental guilt over her assumption that the person was homeless.

Did they know the city was shutting down? What was going to happen to the homeless? Frances forced herself to stop staring and ignored her instinct to go over and talk to the person. She had tried that before only to realize that she was not equipped to offer anything to the person she had approached. What could she do?

She walked out the glass door of the museum and hit the Lyft button on her phone, calling the next available ride to the Buena Vista. Frances was not going to waste her time on a bus right now. Plus, was she exposing herself to COVID-19? Had she already? There were so many people in the museum. Would the busses still be running? Should she go home and get her truck? Maybe. What did one do in a situation like this? She wanted to talk with Sam. Without hesitation she hit Sam's number again and listened as it rang once and went directly into voicemail. "Call. The world is crazy. Love you."

Her heart hurt a little as there was no response from Sam. It had taken some period of training for Frances to learn not to call Sam any moment she felt like it. Sam convinced her to focus the energy in an email or text. That way she could get to it without offending anyone during a meeting. Frances had gotten extremely good at sending suggestive texts in code to Sam—so good that Sam had been forced to get a phone case that covered her screen. Frances laughed about how private Sam could be and the fact she was quiet and adorably shy. The laughter faded as it dawned on her that this communication protocol was really a one-way street. Sam called her anytime she had a minute. She called. Not a text or an email. *I need to think about this and get some input on this from her crew.* The thought threatened to fly out of her brain as a person walked past with a fresh cup of coffee.

"Frances, control yourself," she said, slightly concerned about how easily distracted she could be by the smell of coffee or shiny things. She felt the grumbling in her stomach again. She would get some food at the Buena Vista. She checked her phone and no one else had responded to the BV roundtable request. That was their code to drop anything and everything that was not life-threatening and meet at the round tables of the Buena Vista. It had not been used much. This was not a cry wolf situation. Was it? Where was Cheryl? That woman was usually the first to RSVP to a request to have a drink in the middle of the week during working hours.

Frances realized that the grey Prius that was slowing to a crawl was most likely her Lyft. There were a couple of groups huddled around, checking their phones and trying to get a glimpse of the license plate. Her phone vibrated and she saw that her driver had texted. Wow. That was awesome. It was it her Lyft. She squeezed between the parked cars and made sure to double-check the plate. Molly had given everyone a stern lecture on using ride apps after they traced one of the horrid murders she was investigating to a mistaken ride. Yup. This was her responsible climate ride. She climbed in back. "Fastest route to the Buena Vista Café on the corner of Hyde and Beach, please," Frances said. He had been so quick she hadn't finished typing her destination into the app. She turned her attention to the view outside her Lyft bubble.

The world appeared the same as always. Filled with people headed everywhere and nowhere. Frances noticed that the shops seemed full and the sidewalks were louder and more crowded than normal. Or were they? What was real in this world?

Her phone began vibrating in her hand. Still transfixed by the view out the window, Frances accepted the call. "Hey. Frances here. Speak."

"I haven't talked to you in several weeks and that is how you answer the phone? What if I was some serious art collector or something?"

"Well, then they would believe the eccentric artist is so busy creating that time is special and I must order everyone around. Hey, Molly. I didn't recognize the number. I'm in a Lyft, and you'd be proud—I checked the license plate and driver's name, and I'm tracking the ride. Are you calling from the police station?"

"Again. We need to work on your phone etiquette. I'm calling about the roundtable. Is this a real thing? I'm rather busy at the station right now as we are all being pulled in to figure out how to enforce the stay-at-home order."

"I figured if we are all going down the rabbit hole we might as well do it happy. Is it okay I'm headed to get an

Irish coffee? I know the city is closed or closing or something like that?"

"Rabbit hole? Interesting choice of words. I think the world has opened up and we are falling into the deepest trench possible," Molly said. Frances couldn't tell if Molly was laughing or crying.

"I thought I saw a giant rabbit on the rooftop terrace at SFMOMA today. Turned out it was a toddler wearing a bunny hat. But *then* I saw it again, and it *was* real—it was someone's emotional support bunny."

"Peculiar. I'm afraid I'm not going to make it, but you have an Irish coffee for me. Let the gang know it's okay today. Not sure what all of this means. When I know maybe we can hold a conference call or something. It might be nothing and we'll be back at the Buena Vista on Saturday."

"Hope so. Take care, Molly." Frances wanted to slap her forehead. She felt like she had told Molly to have a V8 vegetable juice. Who said things like that? Frances felt the warmth rising in her body, and she acknowledged both the spark of passion and the peace of safety she experienced when talking with Molly. "Oh, Molly if you only knew," Frances said aloud.

Frances leaned her head back into the sensible gray cloth seat of the Prius and shut her eyes hard. Did she miss an opportunity? She wanted to tell Molly that she'd been painting some amazing work and before she could get further into that rabbit hole, she saw the line of tourists waiting to board the cable car. Oddly, she felt comfort in the familiar line of people waiting to ride the Rice-a-Roni sales object.

"My stop. Wow, you did get me here quickly," Frances

said as she opened the car door and jumped out into the world of people again. She looked up at the neon sign of the Buena Vista and felt her world turning more right-side up. As she looked in through the windows, she could that there were open tables.

"What are you waiting for, lady? An engraved invitation? You're the one who called the roundtable. Or was it a sky-is-falling sort of fake-out so Frances doesn't have to drink alone?"

"Cheryl!" Frances threw her arms around Cheryl, pulling her into a strong bear hug.

"Okay. That's a new one. Oh, shit? Is something really wrong? Is it Dana?"

"Why would you think it was Dana? Did you not see that Dana was the first to text the group about the city being shut down? The whole fucking city is being shut down over a pandemic. By the way, I am not playing that board game anymore." Frances held up her phone and showed her the message she'd received about staying at home as if she was building a case.

"I didn't scroll up. I was in a meeting and all I focused on was drinks in the middle of the afternoon," Cheryl said. "Let's go get a table and order before they really do shut down."

When they walked into the familiar sounds of Irish music filling the Buena Vista, Frances wanted to break into song. Instead she headed toward the closest empty round table, claiming it for the group. Cheryl had stopped at the bar and ordered Irish coffees. Before Frances could get comfortable, Winter was walking toward them with a strange look on her face.

"You're fancy today. Looking hot in that pantsuit,"

Cheryl said. "Personally, I don't love pantsuits because they make me wonder if the wearer is hiding cankles."

"Bite me," Winter said and turned toward Frances. "You need to stick up for the pantsuit-wearing woman. Have you not seen Sam in her Armani suits?"

"You're not in Armani—"

"Cheryl, you might want to double our order," Frances said over her shoulder. She did not want an argument between those two over fashion. It was not what she wanted to focus on as she looked down at her purple yoga pants and hoodie. She breathed a sigh of relief as she realized that Cheryl was out of earshot of the comment or ignored it.

"Hey, Winter, I heard from Molly. She's at the station as they are trying to figure out what is going on—before Cheryl gets back, I need to show you something." Frances took out her phone and pulled up the photos she had taken of her latest paintings. "Do not say a word. This is one of the reasons I'm not letting anyone come over."

"Has Sam seen these?" Winter asked.

"No. She's been delayed in Seattle and then had some side trip to Portland for her latest client. I haven't seen in her since the first week in January."

"Are you counting the days, hours, and minutes? How? What?" Winter asked.

"I have no clue."

"Those paintings are...Frances, those paintings are intense and even I can see they ooze sensual passion."

"I know."

Cheryl dropped back into her chair. "Hope it's okay, I ordered us some appetizers and desserts—yeah, carbs!

I figured it would be a good idea since this might be the end of the world as we know it."

"Are you clairvoyant?" Frances asked as the R.E.M. song came on over the loudspeaker. "Want to sing along?"

"God, no. Frances, don't sing. I'll pay for your first Irish coffee if you promise not to sing," Mary, their favorite waitress, said.

"Mary, are you guys closing?"

"Don't know. We are not exactly sure what any of this means. But you girls sit down and enjoy. I've got something special for y'all to try."

"I'm excited and promise I won't sing," Frances said.

"Who else has answered the siren's call for afternoon drinking over the zombie apocalypse?" Winter asked.

"Dana. The boys are down in garlic town. Molly's working. Sam's in Seattle or Portland, not sure."

"Are we having our last supper at the Buena Vista? I would prefer somewhere a little more—"

"Watch it, Winter. I'm right here," Mary said as she placed six Irish coffees on the table. "Already have your order in when you three get through these. None of you are driving, right?"

"Took Lyft. Thanks, other Mom, and will hopefully have one to take home," Winter said.

"How's toddler Autumn these days?" Cheryl asked.

"She's brilliant and I am so glad to be back at work to get a rest. That girl is going to be going to MIT before she's six. Honestly, she scares me. I can't keep up with her. I went to read *Curious George* to her last night and she took the book and read to me. When she was done, she asked for something a little more fun and challenging."

"Holy shit. The last time I saw her she was still drooling and crawling around on the floor," Cheryl said.

"Cheryl, she informed me yesterday that she was a big girl now and she was ready to use a stove that gets hot and drink some wine—aka, as you grown-ups call it, 'happy juice.'"

"No. She did not say 'aka happy juice'?" Frances said, trying not to have her sip of Irish coffee come out her nose.

"She did. I was not fooling her when I told her I am drinking happy juice." Winter took a sip from her Irish coffee. "I can see it now. I come home from this and she's in the living room with a crew of other toddlers and they are doing an intervention on my parenting skills or lack of skills."

"Sounds like Russell is starting to rub off on her," Frances said. "Or it's in her genes as we are all here drinking our own form of happy juice." She mumbled into the sip of her second Irish coffee. "Keep up, you two. Cheers." Frances raised her clear glass coffee mug with the magic elixir and took a long slow drink of the now cooling Irish coffee. "This tastes stronger today."

"What have you eaten in the way of real food?" Dana asked. "Now, don't y'all go cackling and hooting at once. Yes. It's Dana and I left my precious Banana Belt in Marin to come to the gray skies of the city and the roundtable during a pandemic that could kill off my whole generation. What's it gonna take for a retired AP biology teacher to get a drink around here? And this better not be my Robert Scott moment."

"Scott?" Winter asked.

"The son-of-a-bitch who led a group to their death in the Antarctic."

"Dana, I am not Robert Scott. Now you have me completely freaked," Frances said.

"Frances, this is a virus and who knows? I could be an asymptomatic carrier. No one knows. Chances are we are okay right now, but I highly advise not going out after today."

"We have fallen down a rabbit hole," Frances said and took another drink of her Irish coffee.

2

EMPERORS OF OUR OWN FARMS

"So I wasn't dreaming, after all...unless—unless we're all part of the same dream."

—ALICE, IN *THROUGH THE LOOKING GLASS*

FRANCES SAT DOWN on the cold concrete floor of her loft and studied the newspapers she was using to protect her floor. The papers were all from the past week, and she had heisted them from the lobby downstairs. It was a scavenger quest that she justified for herself with the following logic: If the person who actually ordered the newspaper wanted to read these papers, they would pick them up. The papers stacked up in the lobby, unread, and therefore Frances felt they were a resource that she could use. A smile crossed her face as she realized her symbolic logic professor would be proud of her sequence of argument and support for stealing. She had never been confronted by anyone for taking the papers. She mainly used them to protect her floor from her paint splatters. Today though she was actually reading the stories in the paper. The headlines were about COVID-19 and the world shutting down. She rested her chin on her knee and read one story after another.

Time lost all coordination for Frances. Last week made no sense. Or was it longer ago that they had met at the Buena Vista and talked about what it all meant? Dana had hitched a ride back to Frances's place and they jumped into her truck and headed to the closest Costco for supplies. They were lucky. They had beat the rush and found toilet paper, water, cleaning supplies, and food. Dana focused on protein sources. Frances took her direction from Dana and followed suit. After shopping, she'd taken Dana home and didn't get back to her own place until after midnight. It wasn't until she flopped down on her bed that she realized it was the first time that she had not heard from Sam in over twenty-four hours. She attempted not to panic and was relieved when she saw an email in her inbox. It was cryptic and Frances decided not to respond immediately.

The days since had turned into a blur. She and Sam talked multiple times a day and often ended the evening on FaceTime. Frances would tuck herself into bed and fall asleep cradling her phone on the pillow next to her. Sam was busy but her work was up in the air as Seattle and the state of Washington was stopped. Sam shared with Frances that when she had gone out for a run in downtown Seattle it was beyond eerie. No one was out. Not even the homeless. She did not know where the people had gone. Everything was closed. She was relieved that she had rented a condo instead of staying in a hotel for her latest gig. She could not imagine being in a hotel as COVID took over the city. They were both scared and talked about what they were seeing and not seeing. Frances had not gone out at all. She was lucky and Dana was correct. She was built to be a hermit.

Frances flipped through the pages of the paper and found herself falling deeper into sadness. The stories were heartbreaking and frightening. A microscopic virus was dominating humans and closing countries around the world. Time was not tracking for Frances anymore. She could not remember what it meant to have a Monday or a Thursday as the news blended all the days into one long running story of horror. The virus, COVID-19, had taken away normal life or maybe it ripped off the illusions of normal. Time was no longer marked by a calendar or days. Now time was marked by daily TV updates from California's governor, Gavin Newsom. The news often referenced New York Governor Andrew Cuomo's daily updates as cases were soaring there. Trump was a near-daily presence too. Every time Frances thought of the orange man, she felt like vomiting into a FedEx box and shipping it to him. Not a good idea as she would probably be arrested.

Time was definitely different as the city, then the county, followed by the state, and now most of the West Coast was shut down. Frances paused from the overwhelming accounts of COVID-19 and looked out the window. She stood and walked to her view and from her location realized that there was no way to reconcile what she was reading and learning from the news with her world outside. The sky was actually blue, a Disney blue with birds flying, and the buildings were still there. She half expected a Disney princess to come skipping down the street. Then she noticed the street and what it was missing. Her street was missing people and cars. There was no motion. It was a still-life photo. She looked beyond the rooftops to the small section of Highway 101 she could glimpse from her apartment and had to question her ability to see as there again was nothing. No cars. No motion. A shiver ran down her spine as it was hitting her again.

She turned to the paintings she had put to the side since the closure and getting herself set up to be inside for an extended period of time. The estimate had been two weeks, but Dana had been keeping everyone up to date and suggested that they all plan on at least a month. Frances had turned into a couch slug glued to the TV. It was not that she did not think about working. She did all the time. When she picked up her paint or paintbrush, she was confronted with something else that was causing her to think too much.

The only excitement that hit close to home was when Molly had unexpectedly stopped by, and Russell and Simon were thankfully roasting some hot dogs and burgers on their Green Egg in the parking lot. The people below them complained about the smell of the smoke from the Green Egg coming into their unit so they decided to move it from their balcony to the parking lot. Frances had used the excuse of not wanting to break the safety bubble of her place to keep everyone out. Part of her really wanted to see how Molly would react to the paintings, but once again she'd blown her chance to show Molly what she had inspired. Whatever was happening inside the paintings took a back seat to the world that was happening outside Frances's loft. Molly did share some good news. The virus seemed to have stopped the serial killings that had hit the city over the past two years. It was a strange positive.

Frances stood up and stretched. Her main form of

exercise was the walk from her bed or couch to her kitchen. At one point she thought about not using her remote for her TV, so that if she wanted to change her channel she would have to stand up and physically change it. Problem with that was she could not figure out where the buttons were on her new TV. This was also a difference in her world. Before the stay-at-home order, she rarely watched TV. Now it was on almost twenty-four hours a day. She turned up the volume and said hello to her new friends on the *Today* show. "Cheers, Hoda, what are you going to share with me in this sixth hour of the *Today* show?" It had occurred to her that whenever she turned the screen on these people were always there. How did they do that and where did they actually live?

Frances turned her focus to her best coworker, her espresso machine. "I want you to know that you are an amazing coworker—you'd make it to my main channel list on Slack," she said to the machine as she pulled another espresso shot. "I think I need to give you a better name than machine. How about Carl? With your stainless steel and strong lines, you look like a Carl to me."

Shit. Frances realized that she was now humanizing her kitchen appliances. She looked from Carl to the stove and then her fridge. Would they be jealous if she didn't name them and thank them all for working to keep her comfortable? She set her cup of dark espresso down on the counter and walked to the fridge and gently caressed the handle. "You shall be known as Florence. Flo for short. It's because of your red letters," Frances said and then went to the stove and laughed at the name that popped into her head. "Queen of Hearts, I promise to always keep you clean. I'm sorry I have not brought you a pig recently. It's just me for now." She smiled at her red oven and walked to the dishwasher and gave it a gentle tap. "Tweedle Dee, you have been with me from the start. I appreciate you keeping my dishes so clean on your terms. I promise to not threaten you with only using your twin, Tweedle Dum, the sink."

Frances smiled and thought about setting up a Slack group for her appliances. A direct channel where they would communicate in the digital world. Would she really want to know what her fridge or espresso maker were thinking? Would they go on strike? She picked up her espresso cup again and raised it in a toast to her subjects. "I am the ruler of kitchen appliances. I empower you all to keep working to the best of your abilities." Frances took a sip, savoring the hint of caramel mixed with a toasty biscuit from this latest blend of coffee beans. "Delicious. I know I might be going crazy, but then aren't we all mad here? I wonder if this is what happens to those people who start using tinfoil for interior decoration and protection from the mind rays."

The television blurted something out about jobless claims, and apparently a shark was going to come on and talk to people about money. The comment made her pause and tilt her head. A shark talking about finance and helping a person? Interspecies help was rare indeed. Then she realized it was a celebrity from the show *Shark Tank*. Frances walked over to Flo and pulled out some whipped cream. She had splurged on the special canister at Sur La Table. If she was going to put cream on her coffee, it had better be good and made fresh. It was a treat that she allowed more often now. As the canister worked its magic to form a luscious, cone-shaped cap for her espresso, she thought about her inability to recall what day it really was.

Another strange behavior she observed in herself was talking to god. What the heck was that about? Yes, she had spent years in Catholic school, but her parents, rigid followers of the rules of the church, had recently excommunicated her from the family. Brandon, her older brother, made sure to point out that the church had made them do it. Did it really matter? Would the god she'd been conversing with lately be so strict with the club rules? Religion really was a club. You were either a member or you weren't. Did it really matter at this point?

Yes, she thought, I am alone in this loft, with no need to go out for any reason. Was it easier to say she was talking to God than to herself? As she started down her mental wandering about God, she heard the familiar barnyard wail of a cock-a-doodle-do. Was that a rooster? No. Impossible as this was the middle of the city. She stopped all motion, including her breath, and listened. It couldn't be a rooster—it was late afternoon—and if there was a rooster it would be done with the duty of waking everyone up at the break of day. There were no roosters. Or at least she did not ever remember hearing one before.

Frances continued to listen. She tilted her head—first to the left and then the right. This was a curious habit she had picked up from the family dog. Silence pounded out that she was crazy and imagining things as the humming of her main Slack channel coworkers filled the silence. This was crazy talk. A rooster? What would Dana say? Unless someone recently hired an emotional support rooster. It was impossible. Frances sat down on her couch and laughed about Beatrix the emotional support bunny—not a bunny, Beatrix was a giant something.

She turned to the get ready to watch TV and let her brain go quiet. Still she knew that she had heard a rooster crow break through the silence of the shutdown like it was in the loft with her. It did occur whenever she was getting ready to watch TV. Maybe it was a spirit trying to warn her about watching too much TV. She'd binged through *Pitch Perfect* not once but twice. From the Bellas she went to Bella in *Twilight*. Would COVID-19 impact vampires? If it did come from bats would they be at risk or since they were the undead—would Dana entertain the topic? Probably not as she said the *Twilight* saga was annoying teenage sex rolled into an Anne Rice imposter. She was ready to watch Frodo and his band of misfits make it through their quests. But then she had promised Dana that she would get through *Downton Abbey* so they could discuss it over tea and crumpets or something like that on Zoom. There was not enough time in the day or night to binge through Frances's list of binge-worthy programs.

From her sofa she looked beyond the TV to a rather large section of her wall devoted to yarn, waiting for her to complete projects. It was organized with luscious vibrant colors at the top, moving in an ombre pattern down to the earth tones and eventually a two-foot section that was dark, almost black. As she looked at her organized hoard of yarn she likened herself to a yarn dragon. One that Smaug, the dragon guarding treasures of gold and jewels, would understand. Yarn to her was to be hoarded and protected in all its soft lusciousness. Kept forever young in the skein and not woven into anything but sitting and waiting with the promise of beauty. "Shit. I need to figure myself out." Frances pushed play on the next episode of *Downton Abbey*. Man, how she wished she could sit across the kitchen table from Mrs. Patmore and get her take on baking. One distinct difference was Mrs. Patmore did not have a Carl or Flo in her kitchen; Frances realized Mrs. Patmore's Cuisinart was named Daisy.

As the opening credits settled her into a different level of calm, a return to a new group of friends, Frances couldn't shake the feeling that all of this was some rather epic nightmare and she was going to wake up and it would be all gone. Or at least that was a hope she could hang on to and there was no one there to tell her she was wrong. Sometimes she referred her TV as Jabberwocky. A most fitting name for the looking glass which was her only window into the outside world other than her smartphone, iPad, computer, and Zoom chats with the gang. The Jabberwocky, a wicked creature, spewed out the energy of destruction and death at the hands of people behaving badly in a pandemic. Did these world leaders denying the pandemic comprehend that they were now working for the Grim Reaper? Maybe they did, and that was something they all needed to consider. When the truth was that horrible, people had a tendency to think of illusions to fool themselves into thinking that they had no personal power. That all of these external forces were impacting their lives.

"This crazy thinking needs to stop. I am so lost, and I feel so crushed without Sam." There it was again. The distinct cock-a-doodle-do of a rooster echoed through her loft. It was followed by the bleat of what sounded like a goat. "Now I know I am going crazy. Not only do I think I am hearing a rooster, but I also think I am hearing a goat."

Frances muted her TV and sat as still as she could. Silence was echoed back at her. Could a child be playing with a game? No. Those sounds came from real animals not the Farmer in the Dell game. It was so quiet she could hear her fridge, Flo, keeping her cream cold. She turned the sound back on her TV and realized it was the noise from the TV that she was trying to replace. The sounds of San Francisco that had disappeared overnight.

Another cock-a-doodle-do echoed through her loft. "What the heck?" It sounded like a rooster was standing right outside her loft door. Frances bolted up off her couch and headed for the door leading to the hall. Was she being gaslighted or haunted? Had her building been a slaughterhouse at the turn of the century? This forced her to pause as she waited and realized her heart was beating faster and high enough in her chest she could feel it in her neck.

She stopped herself from opening the door and dialed Simon's number. She was thankful that she could no longer hear the ring or conversations through their shared wall. In the latest remodel the boys had added some soundproofing to the loft. They claimed it was nothing personal and they could not hear much of anything except the piano, but she suspected it wasn't a coincidence that this remodel happened after she started having a lot more fun with Sam. She also knew they were being polite because one morning she contemplated out loud if she should put a silk blouse in the dryer and heard a resounding "Don't ever put silk into the dryer." That was followed by a knock at her door and the boys doing an intervention to rescue the silk blouse and take it to their dry cleaners. The soundproofing came shortly after that episode.

"Hey, Simon. I know this is going to sound strange, but have you heard a rooster?" Frances started to bite her thumb nail. She could hear the house music through the phone and was glad that the soundproofing worked both ways.

"Say what? We were having an impromptu dance party."

"Sorry. Didn't know you were having a party."

"Russell and I are the party. We are both scared to death to breach our bubble with our compromised immune systems. You know, this is a flashback for us. I was just a kid, but I remember when AIDS hit the world," Simon yelled into the phone. Frances heard the music fade and knew he must have turned it down. "Now, what were you asking? Do we have any chicken? Are you in need of meat? I don't think we have any chicken right now. We do have sausage though. Didn't think you were into sausage."

"Funny. Not the question. I asked if you have a rooster in your place or have you heard one cock—"

"I do have a cock. Maybe you need to review your basic anatomy."

"Stop being obtuse. I'm serious. I keep hearing the distinct sound of a rooster. It sounds like the rooster is in my loft."

"Well, do you have a rooster?" Simon asked.

"No. Absolutely—at least I don't think I do," Frances said, looking around her loft. "Unless this is a ghost rooster that is haunting me. It seems to crow the most when I am starting to watch TV."

"Well, Franny pants, we have no chickens, but we might have an African swallow."

"Should I be asking you where you got the coconuts?" Frances loved Simon was an even bigger fan of Monty Python than she was, and it was exactly the humor she needed.

"You were to only eat two to three of those gummy bears at a time. Three tops."

"I'm serious, and I still have your gummy bears. I was going to share them with Sam," Frances said, relaxing a little and taking in a deep breath.

"Really? Do you think Sam would eat a pot gummy? My insight into your woman is that she would not."

"You are probably right and seem to know her better than I do. Seriously though, I heard a rooster outside my door. And earlier I thought I heard a goat."

"Frances, I want you to sit down and tell me honestly. Are you drinking? Or are you sniffing paint thinner again and need to open your windows and get some fresh air?"

Frances was chewing on the end of her hair when a cockle-doodle-do cracked the silence. "Did you hear that?" Frances asked. "That was a rooster and it sounds like it is in our hallway."

"Did you open your door and look?" Simon asked.

"No. What if it's a ghost rooster?"

"Really? Frances are you...Do you want me to go look in the hall?"

"Would you? And report back to me," Frances said and put both hands on her mobile phone.

"Hang on." Frances listened as Simon shouted to Russell, "I'm going to go check the hall for a rooster. Frances believes she heard one in the hall. Now Frances, are you hearing any other barn animals?"

"Not at this present moment but I did hear a goat or sheep or something too." Frances could hear Simon opening their door out into the hall.

"Clop, clop, clop, clop. It looks to be a horse and a couple of Britons. Halt! Who goes there? Hey, Frances, no roosters or goats—it appears that it is Arthur, son of Uther Pendragon, from the castle of Camelot and his trusty servant Patsy."

Frances let the laughter that had been missing from her life explode. She couldn't formulate words through her gut-splitting laughter. "Who—" She dropped her phone she was laughing so hard.

"Frances? Are you all right? Do I need to get you some oxygen? Come to the hallway," Simon said, now joining in her infectious laughter.

Frances managed to walk-crawl the last few feet to her door, where she could now hear both Simon and Russell howling in the hallway. She opened the door and attempted to grab some air, which resulted in a laughing hiccup-snort. This snort sent the three of them into more slap-happy hysterical laughter. "If I don't stop laughing, I'm going to pee my pants," Frances said, sliding down to the concrete floor of the hallway.

"It's okay, we have a mountain of toilet paper thanks to Dana," Russell said, wiping away his tears of laughter.

"It's good to see you two. I can't believe we live next door and have not seen each other in a week," Frances said.

"Now who's being funny?" Russell asked.

"I can't take credit from Monty Python, but the moment spoke to me and I was channeling the *Holy Grail*," Simon said as he sputtered through his waning laughter fit.

"I miss us. All of us," Frances said.

"Yeah. We haven't seen you since that first week everything was closed in March. It is now April tenth," Russell said.

"What? Wait. No. This is the fortieth day of March. I was thinking I was going crazy."

Russell jumped up in the air and did a full pirouette, landing softly on his feet. "You don't have to go crazy as we are all mad here. You two might be Monty Python—"

"Why? Why are you not dancing on a stage when you can go from standing to that with no effort? And don't you be passing judgment. I love Alice and her Wonderland too. If you're going to quote the cat you need to do it with that wonderfully wicked smile," Frances said.

Frances scanned the hallway. "No signs of any rooster? It sounded like it was right at my door. This is bizarre. What the fuck is making that sound? At first, I thought it was commercials on TV. But Jabberwock really is running nothing but Netflix and my movies, so there are no commercials. I haven't watched *Babe* or any other farm animal movies."

"Jabberwock?" Simon asked.

"I named my TV after the Jabberwock from Tim Burton's version of *Alice Through the Looking Glass*."

"Um, Frances—"

"Simon, I'm afraid I might be crazy. I realized that I was taking my appliances for granted and I named them. Wait." Frances looked from Simon to Russell and then back to Simon. "Why are you two looking at one another that way? Hold on—I've seen those looks before. What are you two hiding?"

Frances watched as Russell and Simon continued to communicate without words, in that infuriating way of couples who have been together forever. "What are you two up to?"

"Frances, we have a confession." Simon stood up and walked into their loft and came out holding a rooster.

"I knew it! You do have an African swallow. I suppose the Briton is a goat named Arthur?"

"Good name. Wish I had thought of that but keeping in line with Dana, who inspired us with her Doris Day Chicken stories, we went out and got two chickens. We named them Beak Davis and Joan Cluckford. This is Beak Davis. Beak got out and was the one you heard. I had taken Winston out and left the door open."

"Meet Joan," Russell said walking out with another rooster. "In our defense we are not so campy that we would name roosters after two Hollywood divas on purpose."

"You know those aren't chickens. Those are roosters."

"Thanks, Captain Obvious. We know that now. But the names stuck, and they do answer to them. When we picked them up, we saw fluffy little chicks and were assured that they would lay great eggs."

"Who assured you that they would lay great eggs? The guy who saw a couple of cock lovers and knew he had an easy sale? I've got some magic beans and gummies that will give you quite the beanstalk to play on . . ." Frances was in her second hysterical laughing fit as she looked at Russell and Simon holding two roosters. "Did you talk with Dana about Beak and Joan?" She couldn't finish because she was laughing even harder. "You've made this too easy." She took out her phone and snapped a picture and sent it to the group. "Get a load of these four handsome cocks."

"Are you done?" Simon asked, cracking a slight smile.

"Oh no. I am not going to be done for a long time. I can't believe you were going to gaslight me over a couple of cocks!"

"We want you to meet our kid," Simon said as he whistled. Out came a small goat with a pink collar. "This is Lady Ba Ba."

"A goat? You have a goat in your loft? Not only that, the goat comes at a whistle? Did you two channel *Green Acres*? In what world did you think having a farm in a loft in San Francisco was doable?"

"We love brie and eggs and Dana had us totally freaked out that the world was ending, and we needed to be able to make our own food."

"Did not think this one through, did ya?" Frances said and walked up to the goat. "She's adorable. What does Winston think of all of this?"

"He loves them," Russell said. "He heard his name. That roused our sleeping giant. Get ready, Frances, here he comes."

Frances didn't have time to brace for the Winston kisses. She was now flat on her back in the middle of the hallway as Winston, the Irish wolfhound, was busy licking her face. "Don't need a facial now. Thanks, Winston." Frances tried wiping her face off with her sleeve. "Back to you two. What the fuck? You decided to keep your secret farm life under cover and let me think I was going crazy?

No wonder there was always house music blasting out of your place. The goat—the other night I thought I heard a woman screaming outside but couldn't see anyone. It was the goat, wasn't it?"

"Lady B and Winston were playing. We know that this goes against the HOA."

"What the fuck—"

"Frances. Such language. When did you become so cavalier with the F-bomb?" Russell asked.

"I read an article that stated it was a sign of intelligence. Now what the fuck are you two thinking? You are the HOA. You could've told me. I would have been able to tell you the difference between a chicken and a rooster. Now if you had a beaver in your place to chop some wood . . ." Frances was gone in her own laughter.

"This is a lost cause. Come on, family. Winston. Time to go, let Frances up," Simon said.

Before the goat was herded back into their loft, the elevator doors opened, and Frances thought she was going to faint when she saw who stepped out of the dark elevator into the light of the hallway.

As Sam stepped out of the elevator she stopped short. "It appears I am at the San Francisco zoo."

"Now I know I'm dreaming. How did you get here?" Frances asked, sitting up.

"Nice to see you too. I drove down from Seattle."

"Welcome to our little hobby farm," Simon said.

"Are any of these yours?" Sam asked Frances as she walked over and put her hand out to pull Frances up.

"If this is a dream I don't want to wake up. I'm so happy to see you." Frances let Sam pull her up. Once standing face to face, Frances didn't hesitate and threw her arms around Sam and kissed her. Something clicked in her brain and she abruptly stopped kissing and quickly pulled away and pushed Sam backward with more force than she had meant. Russell dropped Joan Cluckford and caught Sam.

"Frances? What—" Russell asked as he gently righted Sam.

"You've been in Seattle. They are seeing so many cases. We can't infect the boys. Oh, my god."

"Frances. Relax," Russell said. "We're okay. Simon and I are probably better off than most because we are on quite the cocktail for our HIV. The twisted irony in all of this is we know how to live with a deadly virus."

"Russell, let's round up the herd and give them some space." Simon started to herd the roosters through their open door. Lady B followed Winston into the loft and hopped up on the sofa with Winston.

"Quite the welcoming committee," Sam said. "I've missed you."

"I'm in shock over learning that I'm living next door to a petting zoo. And you! You were on the phone with me a few hours ago. You didn't think to tell me you were somewhere in Oregon on your way south?"

"You don't seem exactly happy."

"I'm worried."

"Are you going to invite me in?"

"This is your place too. Come on in and I'm—"

"I know. You're in Frances mode. I understand."

"You're about to understand," Frances said and followed Sam into the loft.

"Is this really your loft? Okay. Where is Frances?" Sam asked as she turned to face her.

"Funny. I've been channeling my inner cleaning person. It wasn't that I couldn't clean before, but the world changed, and I guess I needed something to focus my energy on because it seemed strange to create paintings with so many people suffering. The deaths, the people losing their jobs. It—"

"It's a lot. I know. I feel it, and it is eerie to see the cities quiet."

Frances closed the distance between them and wrapped her arms around Sam. She buried her head into her chest and let her tears fall. She felt Sam pull in a deep breath and the two of them stood in the center of the loft crying. Frances let her breathing and tears match the rhythm of Sam's and she felt them merge their pain, their fears. What was going to happen? Frances let the thought hang in her mind as she held Sam tighter. There was no pretending that everything was okay in the world. Minutes passed and the tears ebbed.

"I'm sure I look amazing," Frances said as she looked up into Sam's teary eyes and reddened face.

"You have never looked more beautiful. I love you. These past few months have been harder than I could have imagined. You changed my life so quickly and I am sorry. I was trying to push you away because I realized I have fallen in love with you faster and deeper than I ever thought possible."

Frances covered her face with her hands and tried to stop the snot bubble that was forming in her left nostril. "Don't look at me. I'm truly a mess and I need to go wash my face."

"I love all of you. You could be covered in snot and I would never stop loving you."

"Not the most romantic thing you've said to me." Frances broke the embrace and ran to the bathroom to splash some water on her face. Her reflection in the mirror showed her a face she had not really examined in a month. The woman gazing back at her looked gaunt and paler than she remembered. Her hair was pulled back into a bun, causing her to look more angular than usual.

Frances walked back into the main room, where Sam was still standing, gazing around at the changes to the loft.

"I'm exhausted," Sam said. "I drove straight through, only stopping to gas up the car. It was bizarre as the highway was basically empty."

"Are you hungry?" Frances asked.

"Only for you."

"Sam—I don't—I have not been out of my place in a month. You know that I haven't gone out. This world has been crazy, and tonight was the first time I've seen the boys since Molly came over."

"Molly's been over?"

"When this all started. She came over and we had a social distancing picnic thanks to Russell and Simon and their Green Egg. Why don't you take a hot shower and get into something comfortable and we can go from there?"

Frances realized there was not going to be any grace period as Sam walked over to the giant canvases and was silent. She watched as Sam focused on each one with a silence that screamed she was really *seeing* the paintings.

"These are—Your paintings are beyond beautiful." Sam walked over to Frances and took the towel out of her hand. "Let's make love."

Frances let Sam take her in her arms and they kissed one another deeply and passionately. Frances felt her fear rising and let Sam's touch engulf her in the passion she had been afraid she had forgotten through the distance.

"Shh. I know you are nervous about the virus. I've been self-isolated for more than fourteen days. I worked from my condo and did not go into the office. I was going crazy not being with you."

"You are a risk I am willing to take," Frances mumbled as she was gently pulling the buttons open on Sam's blouse. The red lace bra let Frances know this was indeed planned. Her lips and tongue traced the line between the red lace and Sam's breasts. This was more than she could have anticipated.

She glanced at her paintings as they made their way to her bed. Sam lay down and pulled Frances on top of her. She couldn't believe that Sam was in her bed. Wherever she was a moment ago in her mind she was completely present now, pressing her lips against Sam's, parting them and kissing her deeply. The force was only matched by her desire to feel all of her. To touch and caress her and to bring her to climax and do it as many times as they could until they were spent. There was nowhere she had to be, and this was going to last a lifetime.

"I missed you more than I could say. During our last conversation I realized that all that mattered to me in this world was you," Sam said as she sat up, pulling Frances's legs around her waist. Frances did not want to stop. Something primal came over as she pushed Sam back down into the pillows and placed her leg between Sam's, lightly biting her neck and working her way down to her breast. She could feel Sam wanting her. The doubts that had riddled Frances were not real. This woman had driven more than fourteen hours to be with her in the middle of a pandemic. She felt Sam arch her back and push against her leg as the tensions were rising.

"You know, Frances. Know that you do not need to hide your attraction to Molly from me."

Frances froze and sat up. She wasn't sure what to say.

"Why did you stop?" Sam said, reaching for her.

"What are you talking about?"

"Frances, those paintings are amazing and not about me."

"I don't understand what you're saying."

"You need to let this wall down. I've known before we started dating and before I fell in love with you that you and Molly have some sort of connection. She's beautiful, funny, intelligent, and she was brought into your life at a remarkable time."

"The paintings...you looked at the paintings and then wanted to make love?" Frances asked.

"I've been thinking about making love with you since we said good-bye. I think about you and want to see you, as you are right now, all the time. You're raw, passionate, alive, and so damn creative and beautiful. I know that you're going to be inspired by other people and I want you to let me see beneath the covers of Frances. Let me see the beauty that inspires you too. I trust you."

"Trust," Frances said and climbed under the covers. "You trust me."

"What did I say?"

"Sam. I was scared to show you what I've been painting."

"I know. I saw the look on your face. You really must

never play high stakes poker. You have a heart that won't let you lie. It shows everything on your face."

Frances leaned into Sam and kissed her lightly. "I'm not—"

"Listen. I love you and I know you love me. I can feel your love. We are writing the rules for our relationship, and it would be crazy of me to think that others aren't going to be attracted to you. It is all about how you and I handle the attractions. They can be negative and tear us apart or they can be positive and help us grow together in love and understanding."

"Sam, you are unbelievable."

"How?"

"I feel that you understand the story behind these paintings?"

"Unrequited love. They speak to me of a passion that is felt and not realized. Or acted upon. There is a mystery and caring in those paintings that is several levels deeper than I probably could ever truly comprehend. All these emotions and interactions that you captured concerning Molly are a lesson about how we could either descend into judgment or step back and allow curiosity and life to lead us through the good that is here for all of us. I believe in our love. Has Molly seen your paintings?"

"No," Frances said and let out the breath she had not realized she was holding prisoner in her lungs as she listened and watched Sam process the reality of what she had created.

"Why not?"

"I was afraid. Afraid they wouldn't be understood."

"Understood by her? By me?"

"Both. I showed them to Winter and she had a very

different reaction." Frances stood and walked over to Sam. She hesitated before slipping her arm around Sam's waist. The tension in her body left as Frances felt Sam pull her closer into her. The smell of Sam's hair product was sweet, and Frances leaned her head on Sam's shoulder.

"Frances—look at me. I love you and your creations. I am here. I am here with you. As long as that is what both of us want. I know our relationship is what feels so right to me. I can't think of anyone else in this world that I want to be with but you."

Sam's lips were soft as she gently kissed Frances. The words Sam had shared about wanting to be there translated into the kiss, and Frances felt the waves of love flow through her body. She put her arms around Sam's neck and kissed her deeper. She stopped and looked up into Sam's beautiful eyes. Eyes that were reflecting the deep royal blue of her workout shirt.

"Sam, I was so scared about sharing this with you, with anyone. And then this COVID-19 stopped the world as we know it. All I could think about was you. It was a physical pain being separated from you. Then I felt guilty because I was worried about my show not going forward in New York while people are getting sick and dying. I have no clue what's going to happen."

"At this point we can only live in this moment. This next breath. Don't think about the future—it isn't real. Right now, we are together, and I am so wet and horny. Are you going to deny me?"

Frances smiled and kissed Sam again, gently at first. "Now where was I before we went into lesbian mode and started talking."

"Shut up and make me dance," Sam said.

"This is my kind of love."

3
STRENGTH

"When I used to read fairy tales, I fancied that kind of thing never happened, and now here I am in the middle of one!"

—ALICE, IN *ALICE IN WONDERLAND*

"WHAT AM I going to do?" Sam asked.

"About what?"

"This?"

Frances turned to look at what Sam was pointing at and tried not to laugh. Sam was holding her long hair out and pointing at the distinct color line that now ran through her hair from her scalp. "I don't know what you're worried about. It looks distinguished."

"It is white. Not a pretty silver fox like Paul Hollywood on the *Great British Baking Show*. To which I am now highly addicted—thank you very much for that. It is dull white. Not shiny. Not cool. Not distinguished, as you say."

"What about this?" Frances responded by pointing to her head.

"You're wearing a hat. You always wear a hat. It is the one way you ignore what is going on with those beautiful red curls."

"We can do some creative lighting for your meetings that have to be over video."

"No. Frances. The last creative lighting you did caused the team to laugh for twenty minutes as they accused me of being in a witness protection program or being interviewed incognito on *20/20*. I need to find someone to fix this. Do you think Russell or Simon would do it?"

"I can do it. I paint."

"Frances, you are not painting my hair."

"The word *trust* is coming up for me at this moment."

"Oh my god, are you really going to challenge me with trusting you to color my hair? Knock it off. I'm serious. I have some really important meetings coming up, and I can't deal with this white root problem."

"The good news is everyone is probably in a similar video chat panic. Unless you're bald. The bald dudes really do not have to worry about shag or roots not matching the outgrowth."

"I'm not shaving my hair off."

"Sam, you would look so sexy with a shaved head. Don't get me wrong—you look sexy with long hair. I might need to stop talking."

"I'm going out for a run. Do not worry. I'm going to do at least ten miles. My meetings were canceled for the morning. I need the exercise."

For the first time since Sam had arrived, Frances was all alone in the loft. She walked over to her espresso machine. "Hey, Carl, fire one up. I need a shot of caffeine. Now that I think of it, we are going to make this a double shot." Frances watched as the coffee beans were pulled through hopper by Carl's strong coffee grinder. She placed her cup under the porta-filter and waited for the magic elixir to fill her cup. Frances smiled as she thought about the conversation she'd had with Sam concerning her work. Energy was pulsating through her fingers and she knew she had to paint. It was time to throw herself back into her work. Sam was right. The future was unknown, and to live this moment now was what she was going to do and capture the image she had forming in her head.

Frances took her double shot of espresso over to her work bench and pulled out a clean canvas. She glanced at the latest newspaper she had heisted from the lobby downstairs and noticed the headlines. It stopped her and she felt her heart beat a little faster. Since Sam had shown up she had walled herself off in her love nest and had the luxury of ignoring what was happening outside their protected bubble.

The news was more depressing than anything she could ever remember. The number of people around the world getting sick and losing their jobs from this pandemic were stunning, and there was no end in sight. Not to mention the political horror show happening in the United States couldn't be any worse. Frances realized that Sam was most likely attempting to find a way to deal with this horror too. Her work had gone from consulting on how to open new business offices and stores to procuring ways to keep employees safe. Sam was deep into the world that was hit with the bomb that COVID19 exploded, but she didn't bring her work into their conversations.

These past two days—or was it four?—were over-the-top special, a love fest that proved absence really does make the heart grow fonder or, as Sam pointed out, horny. They held each other constantly and barely parted to eat. Their only true interruptions came twice a day when Frances remembered to feed her sourdough starter, Mary Shelley. Frances smiled as she recalled Sam comparing Mary to an odd toddler pet. There was also a discussion about naming her sourdough starter after the author mostly known for writing *Frankenstein*. Frances wondered why Sam could not understand why people, namely her, named a sourdough starter at all. She played the conversation back through her mind.

"These waffles are amazing," Sam said. "I don't think I've ever had a waffle that tasted so delicious."

"It's Mary Shelley," Frances said as she was in the process of measuring out the flour and water to feed Mary.

"Oh. The sourdough starter."

"Actually, it is the discard from the sourdough starter. You have to take some out before feeding otherwise we would have to move out of the loft as the wild yeast conquered the place."

"Discard? You mean you made the waffles out of yeast poop?" Sam asked.

Frances laughed again thinking about the expression on Sam's face as she said, "Yes, I basically cook the offspring of Mary Shelley."

"A rather morbid and Hansel and Gretel witch sort of story," Sam said as she finished off the waffle.

Frances loved the conversation and the innocence that Sam without her walls would share. Frances felt her laughter and she had to make a mental note to share these exchange with Dana.

This unexpected time with Sam turned what was a sort of isolation prison into heaven. Although, Frances had done quite the job of hiding and downplaying the work she had painted, and Sam respected her art and did not pry, Frances noticed that whenever she wanted to broach something that might be a little prickly, Sam either went silent by stating she had work to get done or she resorted to distracting Frances with passionate sex.

Why did Sam respond to her attempt to talk about her views by cutting her off with work or kissing her passionately? If the kissing started, they were lost between the sheets again and the passage of time was released as they found one another in what Frances felt was indeed the experience of going through the earthly concepts of time. Her creative passions were stirring, and she decided to seize on the time alone to paint the concept forming in her mind. She was more aware than ever that when the creative muse arrived, she must accept the offer. With a deep breath in and long exhale, Frances stood and took in the loft and her present state at that moment. Alone again she could work.

Her loft was now quiet except for the hum of her ever-present sentinel of the kitchen, Flo the fridge. It was a comforting sound, the constant hum that Flo put out into the world, and Frances shut her eyes and thought about the ease of the past few days. This helped her form the images in her mind that she knew she was going to paint. The images confused her a little as they drew a connection from Molly to Sam. She so loved Sam and she had never felt closer to anyone. They'd camped out on her bed and didn't get dressed until today. Frances looked down and realized she wasn't exactly dressed in anything she would wear outside. A loft proved to be a very interesting lab for a young relationship built on distance.

Frances walked to her work and her paints. She touched the canvases she had set out of direct sight. These paintings that had kept her company for so many days as the pandemic had started and she was alone seemed strange stuck into the shadows. Why? Was she attempting to hide? Her memory seemed to be suspect as the end of February and March were merged into a new and strange month. The calendar basically stopped keeping track after March twenty-something. At first it all seemed like normal for Frances. She was alone in her loft working on her paintings. She had a few annoying calls from Nathan telling her that she really needed to get these paintings done so they could dry in time in order to be shipped to New York City.

She moved the paintings one by one out into the light. This was part of her process and what she needed to do to dive back into her work. To tap those emotions that unleashed the power of the work she was creating. As she studied each piece she was pulled to specific moments. Nathan kept coming to mind. He was not happy with her for refusing to move to New York. He had Felipe try to convince her to move herself out there. This was a new Frances, one that relied on her own instincts, and they were yelling at her to create in her own space. This also had her pause on more than one occasion and wonder if she was picking up bits of the crazy world energy or was it a lucky cosmic collision that kept her home and out of the hotspot that became New York City. At this point it did not matter why she had the strength to tell Nathan no. It was good she did.

As she pulled the drying sheets off her paintings she felt the spark for the current painting pushing for expression. She repositioned the blank canvas and started with the palette of oils she had wrapped in plastic to preserve the paint. In her hand the brush traced the body and the beauty of the woman in her mind. The woman that had opened her rush of passion and creativity, allowing her to create every canvas of her show, was was not Sam. The muse she was painting was met here, in this loft. She captured all the thoughts she had the instant she first saw Molly and all the meetings that came after. Her fantasies about what it would be like to kiss Molly, to hold her, to make love. What was she doing? She looked to the door and listened for any sign that Sam was back from her run. Frances felt her heart beating faster and her neck and face flush. She wasn't creating from the passion she held with Sam. Except that wasn't exactly true either. She felt the connection to Sam with the first inkling of the image. She was flushed over the change in her feelings toward Molly. She stood in front of the latest painting and noticed an "E" to the left of the canvas. What was this in— "Ahh!" Frances said.

"Did you figure something out?" Sam asked.

"Holy fuck!"

"Sorry. I didn't mean to scare you," Sam said.

"Don't you dare laugh. Why did you sneak up on me?" Frances said, putting her hands over her face and in the process smudging a dash of dark blue paint on her cheek.

"Sweetheart, I didn't realize you didn't hear me come in. I was not in stealth mode. Sometimes I wonder if you are even in the same dimension the world is in when you are focused on your art."

"Sam." Frances thought about everything she had been working through and realized that she had pulled out all the paintings and they were overwhelming, and she was standing with her current lover in the midst of her fantasies about another woman.

"Do you want to talk about what you are working on right now?" Sam asked.

"Not sure."

"Frances, I let you take my heart. You are the only person I want to spend my time with, and I do not know how else to tell you that I've fallen deeper in love with you than I ever imagined. You are the best woman, person . . ."

"Sam—"

"Can you say the same?" Sam asked.

Frances watched as Sam's gaze fell on the canvases that captured Molly. The silence was screaming between them, and Frances wanted to say the same thing back to her but felt exposed. "I don't want to lie to you, Sam."

"Then don't. It isn't hard. It's rather simple. You either speak truth or you don't. Respect me enough to tell me when you are going to leave me. Don't cheat on me."

"Sam. Stop. Please sit down." Frances hiccupped back some tears as she tried not to cry.

"Frances, I was told that this—"

"Told what? Told by who? Who are you bringing into this conversation about us?"

"I am not the only one with someone else in this conversation. Who have you brought? Molly? Does she even know what she means to you? I'll ask you again, has she seen these paintings? Do you know what she means to you? Do you know what you want? Is she why you canceled your trip up to Seattle?" Sam asked.

"This isn't...Sam, I need you to stay and not walk away."

"Do you know what I need?"

"You need to listen and if we are going to continue, we need to do this together. I can't do this alone." Frances put down her paint brush. She took a couple steps closer to Sam.

"Stay there. I need some distance. Frances, I want to know what is going on here? Have you been with Molly?"

"No."

"Do you want to be with her?"

"Sam, that is a fantasy and she's with Emily now."

"Not an answer to the question I asked. If she wasn't with Emily would we have a problem?"

"No. You're missing—"

"What am I missing? You're making me crazy and Susan warned me."

"Yeah. I could see her warning you." Frances remembered the waves of judgment she'd sensed coming from Sam's friend. "She has no clue who I am or what we are together. She froze you in time with her sister and that past will never let you be in the present moment for her."

"I'm here. But are you?" Sam sat down with her arms crossed.

"Molly entered my life when things were more insane than I could possibly explain. That past was so dark that I wondered if I was going to survive. Molly was a light and a teacher at a time I needed to know that there was something good in this world."

"It doesn't hurt that she is freak'n gorgeous and has one heck of an accent. What is it, British?"

"Scottish. And yes, she is beautiful and smart and strong."

"And I'll ask again? Do you want to leave me for her?"

Frances turned from Sam to the paintings and back to Sam. She stood in the moment and let Sam's words spill into every cell in her body and with them the sharp pricks of pain as the uncertainty that hung in the air between them grew larger. In an instant, as the fear was mounting, Frances felt something quiet, a spark. It ignited first in her heart and then traveled through her arteries and then her veins. The energy from this spark caused her head to feel prickles and the tiny light strawberry-blonde hairs on her forearms stand, the way they did when a thunderstorm was rolling in and the silence before the clap of booming thunder filled her mind.

"Sam. Please let me get this out. It might not make sense and at first it will seem fragmented. I am asking for you to open your mind as much as you can and know that I am here, with you. I love you. I am in love with you. In this space, this crazy, beautiful space, I was introduced to Molly. At that moment I was bound to her to her. I had not understood how and for a while there was an attraction that I mistook as a passionate, physical one."

"You think that attraction is over?" Sam asked.

Frances took a deep breath in and let it fill her lungs and force her to slow down and not respond with the first words that came rushing to her defense. It was not what she wanted nor was it the truth. Yes. She could see the passion that she felt for Molly in the paintings. It took her an instant to realize what was actually her passion and that was what she needed to communicate to Sam. Would Sam listen? Would she not be hurt? Frances realized she was asking more than she had ever asked of any one person. Another breath in and she let the air out slowly. She let her softness come through and not her fear.

"I understand. These paintings are filled with passion—"

"Not only passion. I see love in these paintings." Sam was quick to interrupt.

"You see the love because that is what I share with you. I am so in love with you, Sam. At first, I even separated what I was painting from us. It was about Molly and I, and I thought it was only about Molly. With you here and the latest painting forming in my brain, I realize that you are in all of this. The reason I know how to passionately love is because of the love I share with you. My love for Molly is not our love and I will not leave us for her. That is the short answer."

"What?"

"In answer to the other part of your question, Molly has not seen these, and I don't know how I feel about her seeing these."

"Frances, that tells me you are confused, and I don't know what this means for us."

"Slow down. Put some brakes on and don't jump to linear conclusions. You know that there is no limit to love?"

"What are you talking about? Do you want to be in an open relationship? I made it very clear when we first started dating what my boundaries are and they have not changed. You told me that you would never cheat on me and we were in a closed, monogamous relationship."

"Not what I'm explaining or asking for, and I am asking for you to meet me in this difficult conversation. To slow down and listen. Try not to put up the usual defenses. We think it protects us when actually we are attacking and the attack is to ourselves most."

"You are the one making it difficult. Frances—"

"What? Sam, what about you? Do you want to leave this relationship, and I'm now giving you the out you've been looking for and wanting?"

"How are you turning this back on me. I'm faithful—"

"Not so fast. Have you ever noticed that your rules are one way? You completely separated me from your hive of friends. I don't intrude on that time or accuse you of cheating with any number of those people. One couple made it very clear to me when you all came biking through that they were much better partner material for you. That I was a mistake and they were going to make sure that your error was corrected. Did I cause a scene? No."

"I seem to recall more than a scene. I've apologized to you for that night and the behavior of the group in total. I thought we worked past that and you're bringing it up again."

"I've been trained to not call you in the middle of the day. To text you. But my texts were too revealing—you gave me a sheet on what an appropriate text was and why. You can call me whenever you want. Any time of day or night."

"You're not in meetings, you are just—"

"Don't you say *just painting*. I'm painting—that's what a painter does, they paint. Do you think the ability to create is something I am able to turn on and off like a spigot or a light switch? That when you call, and I stop painting or creating, I can pick it up and dive right back into what I was doing? News flash, it doesn't work that way for me. Sometimes after you call, I am wrecked as far as work for the next several hours. In one instance it was a week before I was able to get back to my work."

"Maybe I need to set you free?" Sam said.

"That's not what I'm saying. Not what we want. Or at least not what I want." Frances walked over to Sam and pulled her into her arms. "Please believe in me and listen. I don't want us to end. I am exhausted and scared, and this is something that is new to me."

"What is new to you?"

"Loving you. I'm honestly and deeply in love with you. Do you believe in me?"

"What do you want me to say? Why do I need to believe you? You must believe yourself. I think that question has your answer."

Frances walked over to her piano and touched the keys without playing a note. The emotions welling up were strange, and she realized that she was no longer afraid. All the fear of showing her work to Sam had built up illusions of disaster and pain. How could those illusions not attack? This was her creation. All of it, from the paintings to her attempt to push Sam away from her with something that was an illusion. Sam kept her alive and engaged and her heart light. Was that why she wanted to push her away? Was it because she didn't really accept herself? She started to push down the keys on the piano and let the music strip away her layers. Sam didn't move. When Frances glanced at her, she almost appeared frozen, a statute in the moment. "You keep me warm. You keep me in love, and I don't want to lose you. But I also have not treated our relationship with the open honesty and with the respect we both deserve."

"Frances, you are struggling with something that I don't understand, and you need to know that I am here, but I'm gone if you go outside this relationship."

Frances stopped playing the piano. She stood and walked over to Sam. She put her arms around her and pulled her close. Sam stayed motionless. Frances studied Sam's blue eyes and searched for the light that could both calm and excite her.

"Maybe don't say anything. Can you meet me in this hug?"

Frances squeezed Sam tighter and waited to feel Sam's arms around her, pulling her in close. She could feel Sam's heart beating fast and as the seconds ticked past Frances held her breath. Her heart was now beating to match Sam's. It was so fast. She wondered if it was going to give out on her due to the pressure of this moment. She closed her eyes. Sam wrapped her arms around Frances, who took a fresh deep breath of air deep into her core and let the new oxygen fill her lungs.

"I wouldn't take a huge breath. I ran pretty hard and am frightfully sweaty."

"Shall we take a shower?" Frances asked.

"After. This conversation needs to continue for us both."

"Come with me." Frances led Sam over to the first painting and turned to Sam. As she stood between the woman in her painting and the one whose warm hand gripped hers, she knew Sam was right for her. Had she ruined this beautiful relationship? "You know you help me see so much more than I can verbalize," Frances said.

"Teach me. I'm here to learn too."

"That makes two of us. I never really thought of myself as a teacher in a relationship. Promise me though that you won't bring Susan into our difficult conversations. I feel her judgment."

"I promise. You feel your own judgment that you project back to yourself," Sam said. Frances led Sam to a chair that she often used to us contemplate her paintings. It gave her an open view of her gallery. The black office chair was a special gift she received from a professor she had at the University of Washington. Her piano and this chair always came with her when she moved. Frances turned to face Sam and dug into her honesty as she started to explain the evolution of the Molly paintings.

"Glance across the paintings and notice the color changes in the backgrounds. Notice the fact that Molly goes from being well-defined in those paintings on the left, and as we progress through all those pieces to the one that I started today, Molly's form fades into the background of the paintings. Her human form is disappearing. There is an evolution in the relationship that I had not seen until today. Actually, I was scared that I had turned into my own psychotic version of Ethan."

"No. You're talking about the guy who was—"

"Yes."

"Frances, you are not a monster. You are not a serial killer. How can you even think you're anything like that guy?"

"Sam, I know I'm not a murderer in this life. But look at what my own self-hate can do. I was trying to wreck us.

We all have a shadow part or darkness. The world population is going through one heck of a lesson right now. Some communities are doing better than others, and this is quite the reckoning."

"Talk to me about Molly and this sensual lust that I see in your paintings."

"There is lust, there is passion, and beauty. There is also domination, fantasy, and fear. As I studied the dark, almost midnight sky color that peeked out from the back of the naked woman painted on the canvas in the last completed painting before the one I started today, the darkness that brought us together was captured in that moment too. It was a dark underlying story. One I wasn't sure I could verbalize."

"In looking at all your paintings together I am able to see something. My heart tells me you are working through so much that I am stuck on the outside and not able to enter. At first—especially with that first painting, which is stunning—I was jealous. You painted with such intimacy, and it isn't me. I wanted to be the woman in that painting. It is like a love song or love letter. Then I hear you talk about the paintings and I find a sense of relief."

"Why?" Frances was curious.

"It ends. Your feelings or fantasy or whatever you are working through has an end. I don't want us to end."

Frances turned to Sam and pulled her face to hers and gently kissed her on her soft lips. She tasted the salt that had dried on Sam's upper lip. "You understand more than I ever expected, and I am grateful for you listening and learning with me."

"Frances, these paintings are going to captivate all who see them."

Frances walked over and picked up her piano bench and carried it over to where Sam was now standing. Frances placed the piano bench in front of the work in progress, sat on down, and patted the space next to her. Frances looked at the paintings and then to the woman who had bravely accepted her invitation to sit and to listen as she worked through the paintings that she had created. As her eyes moved from one canvas to the next, she saw the circle that was created in the beauty of Molly.

Frances spent the next few hours explaining what had happened in those months after she had met Molly. She talked about how the paintings came to life first in her mind and then on the canvases. The first showed an unbridled innocence of lust and desire, almost an awakening to the fact that she really was attracted to women. She contrasted it to the latest rendition of this growing study. With the movements of the paint through the brush strokes, Frances felt her skin turn cold. Her ego was at work and it was not pretty.

Frances turned to check on Sam's silence. What she saw was softness in her face and a desire to know more. She went through the steps and the paintings, giving each their own time. When she got to the second-to-last painting, she hesitated. The painting looking back was filled with a dark, possessive anger. Was she attacking the woman she had been? Did she blame the world and Molly for Ethan's death? For an inability to protect Emily? The other women? The victims of Ethan were also painted into the work. She had not seen them at first. As they sat there, and Sam asked questions about the images she saw in the paint, Frances leaned her head on Sam's shoulder and let the quiet tears roll down her cheeks. Finally, she was quiet with her work, herself, and the woman who had the capacity to love her and listen.

She had wanted to hold back and not share what had come to her mind with the latest painting. Sam's face, curious and free of judgment, encouraged her to be honest. Frances took Sam's hand in her own and rested it on her thigh and at times her fingers tightened. She shared that Ethan Charna had flashed through her brain and, in that moment, she saw how Ethan had captured his victims in his art. He had once told her that she, Frances Olar Kavanagh, was going to be one of his greatest pieces.

As soon as Frances shared the horror of that reality, stuck in the past and gone with Ethan's death, all her fears came rushing back. She shuddered and felt her world start to spin as her body went into survival overdrive. Sam threw her arm around Frances's shoulder and pulled her close. For the second time that day, Frances felt bile rise in her throat and she wanted to hurl everything she had eaten. She felt she was going to faint. What was it that was stuck deep inside? It felt like someone was twisting something sharp and hot inside her stomach. She had worked through all of this and put the pieces of her life together. Here she was sitting in front of pieces for her New York solo show with the woman that wanted to be with her in every way. She looked at the paintings propped up around her loft, her eyes bouncing from one to another and not lingering for long on any one. "Oh my god. How am I going to explain this?"

"You have. I understand," Sam said.

"What do you think Molly is going to say?" Frances jumped up and away from Sam. "What about Emily?"

"You know it isn't going to be an issue. I'm with you and I understand. This is you. These are your creations and your experiences. Do not let guilt, shame, fear enter into what you created. These are your creations. They are presented not to be judged."

Frances took her extended hand and pulled Sam up off the piano bench.

"You have some serious strength when you want to," Sam said quietly.

"Kiss me," Frances whispered.

"I think you might want to invite Molly over and show her these works. But not to justify or explain."

"Would you mind if I spent some more time working through some of what we've talked about?"

"Frances, you do what you need to do. I'm going to go soak in a tub. It has been a while since I've done such a hard run. My body is not thrilled. Come join me."

"I will. Give me a second to capture something."

Frances went to her computer and started to write down her thoughts about the paintings. She started with the first. She glanced over her shoulder at the painting and then back to the computer screen. She started to type her description and found that she was working through a path she had never expected.

In the first painting, Molly was revealed as a strong champion, one shielding Frances from the darkness. Frances stood up from her desk and walked over to stand directly in front of the six-foot-square canvas that held a mixture of pencil and paint as she was constructing and attempting to capture the fleeting muse. A tear formed and her throat felt tight as she struggled to take a breath. There was no way she was like Ethan. She wasn't out to dominate or kill. But could she? Frances turned to the other paintings to place them back in the drying racks her sister, Theresa, had built for her. The latest one she had mostly sketched out and started to paint the morning that Sam had arrived. This was dark. What was so dark? Was it a possessive love that was possibly walking the line of obsession?

"This shit is getting real," Frances said as she walked over to her kitchen island and poured the last few ounces of wine from the open bottle. The bath water was on and she could see steam coming out of the open bathroom door.

"Siri, play my latest music mix," Frances said and walked to her piano. A beautiful soprano started to sing the song "The Wee Small Hours of the Morning," and Frances let her hands go on the ivory keys. Her music had been a place where she found solace and peace. Halfway through the next song, "Empty Chairs at Empty Tables," she realized that the whole world was experiencing this song. Her tears hit her forearms as the tenor's voice hit the crescendo of the song and she stopped playing and listened to the music. What was she thinking when she put this list together?

"Why did you stop playing? You play so beautifully." Sam's voice, like a song to Frances, came through the open door of the bathroom into the loft.

"Any requests?" Frances asked.

"What's that one I love so much? Then come join me in the tub."

Frances smiled and started to play Ennio Morricone's

title song from *Cinema Paradiso*. She mashed that into "Gabriel's Oboe" and then let her mind play whatever came to her. Another day was growing dim as twilight filled the sky, creating a softness that matched the music filling the loft. Frances turned to look at the paintings and felt a new peace come over her as she realized that what she created spoke of a truth she needed to reveal to herself.

4

A PARADOX LEFT HANGING

"No, No!" said the Queen. "Sentence first—
verdict afterwards."

—ALICE IN WONDERLAND

W HEN THE EMAIL evites for the Buena Vista Irish
Coffee Club Zoom call had come in that morn-
ing, Frances was not exactly sure she still wanted to participate. The days merged into weeks and now the weeks
were months. When all of this first started, the Zoom
gathering of the club was different, fun, and surreal. Now
it felt like it was actually squashing hope. That her world
was falling further away from her and, as she tried to
grasp at the threads, they were breaking off, leaving her
with nothing. Not to mention this world in pandemic
and economic chaos did not seem like a world that
allowed one to celebrate. Gone were the noise-making,
singing, clapping for the health care workers thrust into a
war they were told to fight with basically no help. Frances
had heard from a few friends from St. Louis that things
were not going well in that city. Her family had yet to
reach out to her.

The second week in April she had written heartfelt

letters to each one of her family members. When she had talked with Russell and Simon about writing the letters, they suggested she write them but not mail them, then burn them and let the universe send the message. Her family, they said, did not deserve her reaching out to them after what went down concerning her coming out. Frances wrote the letters and Sam encouraged her to send them. She did. The silence was still in place and Frances realized that, unlike some other friends she had chatted with over the phone, she was not going to know how her family members were coping with any of this. She was gone to them and that was it.

Not completely lost though was her connection to her youngest sibling, Theresa. Theresa was living in Monterey, California with Joshua and had not reached out to her. Joshua was so special to Frances, and it took Theresa to point that out to her. Frances was not completely comfortable with their relationship because she did not trust Theresa's motives. As she thought about that mistrust projected onto Theresa, Frances came to realize that there existed some feelings for Joshua that reached into the past when Joshua was Jennifer.

When the world had gone crazy, Joshua had reached out to Frances immediately. To make sure she had food and toilet paper. It was odd. The whole toilet paper shortage in the United States. Did people believe that stockpiling TP would save them from this virus? It was an odd state of affairs, but thanks to Dana and the boys, Frances was stocked with toilet paper for the next year. Joshua had started giving away a roll of his restaurant's toilet paper with each takeout order. It became a joke about his food and so he stopped and donated the supply to a couple local charities. His coffee bar was doing okay. People needed their liquid happiness. A couple people from the Monterey Bay Aquarium came over and painted various sea creatures on the sidewalk to help people with social distancing. It was quite a nice addition. Joshua had texted pictures. His restaurants had been closed for a few weeks. When he'd reopened, the takeout business was so meager he had shifted gears, focusing instead on making sure people did not go hungry in his community. Apparently Theresa had come up with the idea to start cooking soups at first. Then they baked bread and gave away boxes of produce to anyone who needed the food. Now they were making enough meals to feed more than two thousand people a day. Joshua had shared that they were working with the local farmers to make sure that produce was getting harvested and delivered to people who could use it.

Her mind went to some dark places. Sometimes when she closed her eyes, she saw the giant rabbit toddler she had seen in the San Francisco Museum of Modern Art when this bizarre new reality had started. The instant the child turned completely into a rabbit in a flannel plaid shirt, Frances would open her eyes and her vision instantly transitioned her back to her loft. What had she done to make someone else's life better in all of this? What was she doing at all? She looked at her painting and then to her kitchen.

She had ordered takeout a few times and found herself too scared to eat the food. She gave it to Russell and Simon, who were happy to enjoy the meals. She stopped checking her mailbox for any letters from anyone in her family and was feeling rather isolated, lonely and useless as the world fell deeper into the throws of the pandemic.

Her solo show had been pushed back from May to September. Given how poorly things were going in the country, she doubted that her solo show would go on at all.

Frances was so focused on devastation that when she opened the evite from Winter, what she felt was dread instead of excitement. There was something odd and separate about getting together over the computer screens. A disconnect that took her to another place and time when you could be out in the world and not wonder if you were going to contract COVID-19.

Frances reflected on some FaceTime calls with Winter and Autumn that had made her feel like she had been put through a crash course on virtual-reality nausea. She learned to not look at the screen when in control of the toddler. A few times the calls took place with Frances watching the ceiling at Winter's condo. Frances wondered if Winter knew that her daughter was torturing those they dialed up or was completely oblivious. On one call, Frances had suggested to Autumn that her mom was going to let her eat ice cream and candy, and to top it off, told her that she should not go to bed because she would miss playing with the pony. That stopped the calls for a while.

"Sam, do you want to participate in the Zoom call that Winter has put together for the Irish—"

"Do we get to drink real Irish coffee this time? I could order some to go from the Buena Vista and run 'em back here."

"She said she sent us all new kits and they will be here today. I will—hang on, the boys are at the door." Frances peeled herself off the leather couch. "Must remember that leather is not friendly to skin when hot. Ouch."

"Hey, Frances, don't forget we're doing a BBQ with the boys tonight on the roof."

"Why would I forget? It isn't like I have a busy calendar."

"Paddington." Sam using this word on Frances had her stop and reflect. Had she snapped or been rude? *Paddington* was the warning word that she and Sam had come with to help her check herself. Frances loved Paddington, the adorable bear in the hat and car coat—it made her smile. It was the easy hack when things were getting overly heated, which was becoming less and less in the world of isolation. Still, there was something that tipped Sam to use it with her. Frances took a deep breath and kept the smile as she turned to face Sam.

"Sorry. I'm out of sorts. Let me get the annoyance handled on the other side of the door." Frances reached the door and opened it quickly to stop the rapid succession of knocks. She was not surprised or amused to see Russell standing with his right hand ready to knock again. He thought of himself as a genius and would often mimic Sheldon Cooper, from *Big Bang Theory*.

"Where's Leonard?" Frances asked, stepping aside to distance herself from Russell as he entered. "Why do you do this?"

"Do what?" Russell asked.

"She's referring to the fact you are acting out a Calvin Klein men's underwear ad," Sam called out.

"It isn't fair. A man your age should not have those." Frances pointed at Russell's six-pack abs.

"Frances, Franny, Fanny pants, when are you going to learn? As a gay man I am genetically perfect. Not to mention I'm only twenty-nine."

"Really? For the twenty-ninth year in a row?" Sam asked.

"Meow. You can be quite the little pussy snark. I like it. Hanging out with Frances is giving you an interesting edge."

Frances looked from Russell to Sam and back to Russell. It reminded her of a sporting match of some kind, but she wasn't sure if it was tennis or rugby.

"Fairy dust keeps us young and in shape," Russell added.

"That and you must do a thousand pull-ups a day. When I head out on my run, I see you down in the carport doing pull-ups on the bar like a Navy Seal, and you are still doing them when I return."

"Shhhhh—I don't want anyone to know how much effort I put into this bod. It needs to keep the illusion that it is effortless, and I am a god."

"Whatever. What's up?" Frances asked.

"I was wondering if you wouldn't mind babysitting Lady Ba Ba for the day. Please. Please with sugar on top? Please and I'll help you get abs too. Oh, and Molly is joining us for the BBQ tonight. She says she has a surprise for all of us. I do hope it's something yummy. Maybe her aunt made some of that Danish pastry."

Frances had to sit down. Why was Molly coming tonight? This was to be a relaxed BBQ. Not a huge party. "Are you going somewhere?"

"No."

"We need some prep time and she is a most curious little creature."

"Frances, say yes," Sam said as she walked over. "Russell, you really do have an impeccable physique."

"Enough to flip ya?"

"Nope. Like you'd know what to do with me anyway?"

"Okay. You two need to stop this strange sexual banter."

"Frances, you're a bisexual woman. What is wrong with you?" Russell asked.

"I guess I really did not think about myself as anything that defined. You are technically correct, but I have not gone back to men after my divorce from Dickhead."

Frances leaned into Sam, who had thrown her arms around her. "We can take the kid. Although I am still a little confused as to why it is just Lady Ba Ba and not the rest of your zoo."

"Frances, they want to have sex and some privacy."

"You've got a quick one in Sam. Hang on to her." Russell dashed back into the hall and led a very perky little Lady Ba Ba into the loft on a leash. "I would keep her under leash supervision, so she doesn't eat something you really don't want her to eat. They do eat everything."

Russell was gone before Frances could ask any questions about anything. "Do you think she's housetrained?" Frances asked Sam, handing her the pink, bedazzled leash.

"Don't hand her to me."

"You're basically the one who said yes. You've got kid duty."

"Maybe we need to do a mini field trip and take the goat out to my house."

"That's a good idea. She would be able to feel grass under her feet. Hooves? Are those paws? See, I really should not be in charge of anything when I can't identify what type of feet they have."

"Hooves. Goats are actually ungulates, which means they have two main hooves on each foot and are known as cloven-hoofed animals. They might be part dog as they have a dewclaw. Actually, I was thinking she could eat to her little heart's content and take care of my overgrown garden."

"Channeling your inner Dana? Or is there a farm girl in there that I am about to meet? Let's do it," Frances said. "I'll put a picnic lunch together. It will be like a vacation to an exotic location."

"My, how we've changed our ideas of vacation," Sam said. "I really find it amazing the boys created a farm in their loft. Crazy."

Frances got busy in the kitchen. After she finished feeding Mary Shelley her 120 grams of flour and water, she dug through her pantry and Flo, the fridge, putting together a whatever picnic. She stood up and glanced at Carl. She could not remember what the coffee situation was at Sam's place. Her shock at opening Sam's fridge was something that she had not forgotten. It had contained exactly one can of Diet Coke, a plastic container of a pre-made salad, and a half-eaten Snickers bar. That was it. It was almost as if the fridge had no idea it was a place to keep food chilled. Sam's kitchen was beautiful, with black marble countertops, a black sink, and gorgeous maple cabinets that had been stained with a natural gloss. Did she have silverware? Her kitchen was a cook's desert. No condiments and an empty pantry completely devoid of spices.

"Do you want to stay at my place?" Sam asked.

"What about the plans tonight? If we do that, we might want to grab a few more items."

"Maybe when we don't have a kid on a leash."

"Do you want a coffee this afternoon?"

"Frances, is that even a question? Brings me back to the BVICC call Saturday morning—are you more into it today or do you want to skip this one?"

"Let me think about it. Maybe getting out to a different location will give me a different perspective."

"I saw that Molly is going to join the call on Saturday. She RSVP'd. Looks like you are going to have many opportunities to chat with her. Why don't you reach out to her and get this over with and stop fretting."

Frances popped her head above the island countertop where she was fishing out some paper plates. "I didn't look at who accepted. Guess she's able to break away from the cop work. I am getting closer."

"She's up in Portland. Emily's going to be on the call too."

"How did I miss this? When did she go up to Portland?"

"Frances, you need to open your email more often. Molly sent out a group email saying she was taking some time off and was going to self-quarantine and then head up to Portland to spend time with Emily."

A tightness in Frances's stomach made her stop what she was doing and grip the counter. She turned to look and see if Sam had seen her reaction. Why was she not admitting that this news shocked her to the point that she felt pain in her core? This was crazy. Sam was sitting on the floor cradling Lady Ba Ba in her arms and gently humming. Her long hair was pulled back in a ponytail, revealing her beautiful neck and jaw line as she looked down at the goat, who was totally enthralled with the attention.

Frances felt like she was wasting away as the days morphed into weeks and then into months without being able to savor the friendships and the people she loved. She looked at the two reusable grocery bags filled with food and utensils for the picnic at Sam's place and all she wanted to do was jump under the covers on her bed and hide. It was time for her to get out and see the world again.

"Do you want to take Snow White or your two-seater roadster?" Frances smiled, knowing what the answer was going to be. Of course, it was going to be the truck. Sam had teased her about naming her white heavy-duty diesel truck after Snow White until Frances forced her to watch Kristen Stewart as Snow White. It went deeper for Frances and she realized that sometimes Sam stayed in her pragmatic, linear brain as a way to cope.

The time together gave her a new perspective into what Sam did for work. It shocked Frances when she would hear the way some of the senior leaders for the companies that Sam worked with spin a bunch of bullshit. It reminded her why she'd spent so many years of her work life with what she called a zombie brain. The mind-numbing incompetence of those people running companies was one of the first things Frances had selectively forgotten from her former life. To listen to Sam's conference calls brought some of those memories flooding back.

Frances could also see that some of the shield that Sam held up was starting to crack. Her main sponsors were pulling back as the news of the economy and the virus was entrenching itself in the population. Promises that had been made in March were now being un-promised in June with the expectation that Sam would deliver what they had contracted for over several months in a week. Some of it was downright mean, and Frances wanted to scream at those people for attacking Sam for situations they had created.

"Earth to Frances. Ready to go?" Sam was standing in front of Frances. "Hello there, silly? Where were you?"

"Sorry. I was thinking."

"I could see that...Where do you go when you're thinking so hard?" Sam asked.

"Here. Take this bag for me. I'm ready. I'll grab the keys." Frances handed a bag of food off to Sam and walked to the table to retrieve her phone and keys. "Is there anything I can grab for you?"

"Good to go. Still curious—do you travel somewhere when you check out like that?"

Frances didn't know how to answer. She knew she did, and it impacted some people more than others. She had gotten better since she had been painting.

Frances drove them through the empty city streets and found herself wondering if she was actually awake. When she turned onto Third Street she realized that she was taking a roundabout route to the Golden Gate Bridge and north to Sam's home.

"Headed to your church?" Sam asked.

"Have not seen SFMOMA since the day this alternate reality started. I can't believe they are laying off so many staff members. I'm worried." Frances slowed down the truck as she saw the building come into view. The street was completely deserted. No cars. No people. The scene caused a shiver to run down Frances's spine. "Does the building look like it no longer has a soul?"

"Stop it. Frances, you are overly dramatic. The SFMOMA is going to recover. This disease is not going to take us all out, and I wish you would stop watching dystopian end-of-the-world movies."

"Excuse me? Where's the woman sitting in my truck cab, cradling the goat in her arms and humming "Poker Face" to her? I want that Sam back." Frances pulled across the street from the entrance to the museum, put the truck in park, and hopped out. There was no one around. The streetlight at the end of the block had turned from red to green. Frances took in a deep breath and walked to the front of her truck and leaned on the hood. She looked up at the sky and noticed how clear it looked. The quiet purr of Snow White's diesel engine broke the silence of the street.

The lights were off in the museum and the buildings surrounding it. How was it possible that no one was around? How much change could she actually accept and not go completely bonkers? She glanced through the windshield at Sam, who was also looking at the museum across the street.

"Thanks," Frances said. "I needed a few minutes to say good-bye to something."

"What did you say good-bye to?" Sam asked.

"A life that I'm afraid will not be coming back anytime soon."

"You don't know that—no one knows what's going to

happen. It's unfortunate that the disease in this country has been mixed up with the politics of idiots."

"Would you mind if we did not speak of politics and the pandemic for the rest of the afternoon?"

Frances drove them through the carless streets of San Francisco and was relieved when she got onto Van Ness and there were other cars. She felt her heart ache and she wanted to speak about the various tents and homeless clusters and camps they passed on their drive through the city. When they got to the Golden Gate Bridge, it felt good to see the blue sky, the ocean, and a few people walking across the bridge. At 11:00 a.m. in the morning, it was still odd that she could count the number of cars on one hand.

"When was the last time you were home?" Frances asked.

"February."

"February? I thought you were in New York in February and then went straight to Seattle?"

"I had to come home and change out my clothing."

Frances tilted her head and thought back to the month of February. She had missed Sam and told her how much she was craving her. Sam claimed to have the same cravings, but her work schedule dictated she fly directly from New York to Seattle. Frances remembered it clearly because it was one of the times she had called and chatted with Dana about this whole long-distance relationship.

"When we get to your house do you mind if I give Dana a call? I have not chatted with her in a while."

"Tell her I said hello. I'll take Lady Ba Ba into the back

yard and give her free reign. Do you think we should've left a note for the boys?" Sam asked.

"Text them that we're holding their kid hostage in Marin. They'll be fine with it."

Frances found a comfortable overstuffed chair in Sam's study and let herself settle into the softness of the cashmere throw that was draped across the arm and back. Sam had beautiful taste and had decorated her house with colors, patterns, and styles that were softly elegant. It was an adult house. Frances glanced around the room and noted the slight layer of dust that had settled on the bookshelves and the top of the table. It was a gentle message that the room had been undisturbed for a while. The sunlight coming through the large window warmed the room and gave it an added level of comfort.

"Hello?"

Frances felt her heart skip a beat hearing Dana's voice piped into the center of her brain through her AirPods. She needed to remember to turn them down when calling people.

"Howdy, Dana. What's new?"

"Nothing much. I'm harvesting honey right now and that is enough to make me question my own madness. What are you doing? How's Sam? Figured when she showed up you were a goner."

"Sam's good. We're actually at her place and if things were different you know I would stop over."

"Thank you for not stopping over. I do miss you but

I'm not ready to host anyone yet. Did those boys figure out what to do with their coq au vin one and two yet?"

"Dana, you know that Russell and Simon are not going to cook their cocks."

Frances and Dana both laughed over this latest joke. "I can't believe they thought they had purchased egg-laying chickens."

"What about a goat?" Dana asked, taking a breath between her side-splitting laughter. "I've missed you."

"Me too. Sam and I are making out okay. I think we get past some difficult issue and then she pokes me again."

"What are you talking about, Frances? I need a little more explanation."

Frances laid her head back against the top edge of the chair back and looked through the open study door out to the kitchen. She didn't see Sam and figured that she was still outside playing with Lady Ba Ba. "We have had this tension between us. She had gone out for a run and I started work on the latest painting. The result was a personal art showing of the whole collection. To say it was heavy is an understatement . . ."

"You mean the ones you painted of Molly."

"Yes."

"Frances, you need to figure out what you want and be honest with yourself before you can be honest with anyone else."

"Dana, trust me. I'm there. The illusion's fully removed and the honesty and reality exposed. I am in love with Sam. But—"

"But what?"

"She said that she had been here in February. That was the last time she had been at her house. Sam lied to me."

"Did she?"

The way Dana had answered caused Frances to stop and look at her dear friend. There was more to the tone and the way that Dana had posed that question. What was going on here and what was Dana not saying? "She told me that work was keeping her so busy she was going to travel from New York to Seattle and not stop in, and so she couldn't see me. Then to shine things off further, we had an argument over the Molly paintings, and she said that Susan had warned her about me."

"Frances, are you hearing yourself?"

"What do you mean? Dana, I need a friend at the moment. She's driving me crazy."

"If she's driving you crazy, then stop climbing into the passenger seat. What did you think she was going to do when she saw those paintings of Molly? Ignore the message that you've painted so well that any idiot will stop on the first level of understanding and figure out the artist has the hots for the woman in the painting?"

"Not true. Those paintings are a study in—"

"Cut the shit, Frances. You and Molly have an electricity. Even I saw that. But you two decided to pursue other paths. This is an illusion you are continuing because your ego is talking."

"I'm happy with Sam. I'm in love with her. We are two people that are independent and stronger together."

"Are you? People in love—in real love—do not have a substitute. They do not have an inkling that someone else could be changed into the place your current lover is holding in your life. Your ego is trying to substitute a change on you."

Frances stood up and paced the small study. She stared

at her bare feet and wondered if she should have kicked her shoes off so quickly when they entered. She glanced toward the kitchen and out to the backyard. She saw Sam running back and forth across the yard and figured she was playing with the goat. The woman claimed she was not an animal person. Frances shook her head.

"Earth to Frances. Are you really in love with Sam?"

"Yes. I want to marry her."

"Why?"

"Dana. What do you mean why?"

"Why are you questioning her honesty on one hand and on the other you say you want to marry her? Frances, you need to slow down and figure out if you even want to be in the same life with this woman. She's fabulous and you do not need me or anyone else to tell you that. If this is not coming from inside you, from where your love resides, then you need to stop leading her on and let her go."

Dana's words pierced deeply into Frances's soul and her breathing became fast and short. Her hands started to sweat as she thought about life with Sam. "I love her. I honestly am in love with her and can't imagine life without her. I'm scared and I don't want to lose her."

"Have you told her you're scared? Or have you pulled a Frances and spaced off and given her a riddle to solve?"

Frances was silent, pondering.

Dana cleared her throat. "I'm taking my own advice. I'm glad you called but this car ride is over and I'm bailing out of the passenger seat. See ya on Zoom Saturday. I got my Irish coffee kit and I hope I can keep it until Saturday."

"Dana, Winter sent us a fifth of whiskey."

"Exactly! Have you seen the size of my coffee cup? Love you, Frances. Ta ta."

Frances looked at her phone and the call-ended notice. Dana was holding the mirror inches from Frances's face and she was right. There was some serious soul shit to deal with, and it was hard to open her eyes. She was lost in the image of Sam out back and knew that she did not want to change her mind. That was what scared her. What if she really looked inside and the answer was not Sam? What would that mean to her? She had chosen to stay. Was that a choice?

The sky was a beautiful orange and rose ombre as they crossed the Golden Gate Bridge, heading back into the city and the loft. The boys had texted about an hour ago, saying they were going up to the roof to fire up the Green Egg for the BBQ. Winter and Cheryl were going to join them on the rooftop for an adult night out. Winter's latest man friend and his sister were going to tackle the task of watching Autumn. Frances wondered if Winter had shared that she had nanny cams stashed all over her condo. Most likely that was not revealed at this point.

"A dollar for your thoughts," Sam said.

"You wore out Lady Ba Ba." Frances glanced at the sleeping goat on the back seat. "You treat her like she's a dog."

"She's adorable. The boys might not get her back. Seriously. You've not said much today."

"I'm thinking about us."

"I've been thinking about us too," Sam shared.

"That sounds ominous and a little foreboding."

"Frances, you're projecting. I was thinking about how nice it was to hang out and be in my house with you and not be pressured to have to do anything. The food you brought was so good that I don't ever need to eat out again."

Frances tried not to let the tears fall. She gripped the steering wheel so tightly she cut off the blood to her fingers. What was all this about? "I think I'm coming into my period."

"Not an excuse for your emotional madness."

"You said that you couldn't come home in February and you did. Did you forget you lied?"

The silence between them was growing as Frances drove them past the quiet businesses, shuttered for months now. The streetlights were still operating, but there really was no cross traffic and Frances felt like putting her foot to the floor and racing through the city. She'd heard reports that people had been going over a hundred miles per hour through the streets of San Francisco, and she understood the appeal. It was a dangerous thrill.

"It was a change at the last moment. I needed some time alone. It isn't an excuse."

"I would have understood. How would you have responded if I had an opportunity to see you and then didn't? You claimed that you were craving me?"

"Frances, I was and that made it even harder. I was having a really hard time and I needed space."

"That's why I'm here. I thought we were partners, but sometimes it feels like only when it's convenient for you."

Frances pulled into the parking lot to the loft and saw

the party lights on the roof had been turned on. Cheryl's car was in the visitor's spot, and Frances covered her face with her hands. "Arrrggghhh. I hate this," she yelled.

"Me too. Do you want me to head back to my place?" Sam asked.

"No. That is what you do. You leave. I want you to stay. Stay in this discomfort. We need to know if we are changing. You know, Dana said that true love does not bring in substitutes. If either of us are looking for a substitute in this relationship it is because we created an illusion most likely driven by our egos."

"Shit, Frances, can you get any heavier? What the fuck?"

Frances looked at Sam and saw that her eyes were leaking. "You're crying."

"I love you so much it hurts. You scare me. I don't want to lose you and those beautiful, erotic paintings in your loft make me wonder if I ever had a chance with you."

In one move, Frances unbuckled her seatbelt and landed in Sam's lap, kissing her passionately. She felt Sam's arms around her waist and Sam's teeth gently bite her lower lip. "Do you know I thought I lost you and created this whole scenario about why you had not seen me in months?"

"My surprising you here during a pandemic and throwing my pragmatic, linear actions to the wind to be with—"

"Kiss me," Frances said. "We need to go upstairs and fast. I want you and only you. You are heaven."

"I feel that way about you. You are the addition to my soul that helps me see the light in this world."

"It is scary. I see you the same way. Does this make sense? I don't see us as becoming one person. I actually see us as expanding."

"Frances? Do you want children?"

"What is it when lesbians have sex, they get a puppy?"

The two started laughing and both jumped when Winter knocked on the passenger window.

"Hey, ya horny beave hunters. Get a room," Winter said.

Frances opened the door and climbed off Sam's lap. "We—"

"I know what you two were doing. I have Winston duty. He's off watering some tires."

"Man, it's good to see you, in 3D," Frances said, doing the gesture for an air hug.

"Fuck that. You know I've been isolated—get over here." Winter gave Frances a tight hug. "I don't care if you're uncomfortable. You know I get tested like every two days since we found out about Chip's mother having cancer. They are keeping her at home so they can see her."

"I had forgotten. Sorry. That's so rough. How's she doing?"

"All I can say is that it sucks. Her treatments keep getting postponed and they are trying a couple different drugs to keep the breast cancer from growing. Through it all she FaceTimes with Autumn and makes her these adorable little clothes for her stuffed animals."

"Is Cheryl on the roof?" Sam asked.

"She's up there talking about virtual dating. The woman is a freak about it. Thank god you're both here. I think Russell was ready to throw her off the roof."

"Violent."

"Guess who's coming to dinner?" Winter smiled at Frances.

Frances felt like running and hiding. Was the universe really this cruel? Were the gods so bored that they had to bring the situation to an explosive point? Winston was barking loudly at the back door of the truck. "Shit. I forgot we had Lady Ba Ba in the back seat," she said.

"Might have to report you to the police. She'll be here in about an hour," Winter said.

As the information left Winter's lips, Frances turned to see if Sam had heard. She watched as Sam slowly shut the back door after gingerly lifting a very sleepy goat out of the back of the truck. "Did you hear who's coming to dinner?"

"Molly."

"What's going on?" Winter asked as she pointed to Sam and the goat.

"Didn't your mother teach you not to point? A lot is going on and I'm exhausted."

"Winter, do you think you'd mind taking Winston and Lady Ba Ba up? I think Frances and I need to go have a chat."

5
WHERE ARE OUR MENTORS

"It's no use going back to yesterday, because I was a different person then."

—ALICE, IN *ALICE IN WONDERLAND*

THE EVENING WAS warm, with a soft breeze that gently caressed the skin. From the rooftop the Bay and the lights twinkling across lower San Francisco were visible. The ever-changing Bay Bridge light display added to the beauty of the evening. When Frances and Sam climbed the stairs to the roof, they stopped right before opening the door. Frances could hear the laughter and music coming through the metal fire door and her heart skipped a few beats.

"When do you want to share our announcement?" Sam asked.

"Right away," Frances said, looking down at the diamond ring on her left hand. "You are my love and inspiration."

"I understand that now and you're mine."

Frances stood on her tiptoes to reach up and kiss Sam. She took Sam's hand in hers and opened the door and led them out onto the roof. The smell of brisket mixed with the citronella candles brought back strange memories of summer nights before COVID. She smiled at the gathering of her closest friends standing at sporadic distances. The conversations were a little louder, the music a little lower. When she saw Molly and Emily sitting on the picnic table bench facing the boys, she felt a both jazzed and relieved when Sam squeezed her hand. Frances looked into Sam's deep blue eyes and knew she was home.

"Look who made it safely back from Marin. How was your trek to the north county?" Russell asked, giving them both an air hug.

"It was good. Lady Ba Ba is sleeping soundly in her pen."

"Thank you. We needed a break from that little energy vampire." Simon winked at Frances. "Kids are so much work."

Frances walked over to Molly and Emily, still hand-in-hand with Sam. "Hey, strangers. Wow. What a surprise."

"A good one I hope," Molly said.

"Thought you were up in Portland?" Sam said.

"I was. We wanted to be with our friends. We basically got back seven days ago. Time is so strange right now. We were tested for COVID three days ago, and it came back negative this morning. I hope you don't mind we crashed the party. We've got some news we would like to share with everyone in person."

"Y'all are part of this mad party and you could never crash it—"

"Frances has channeled her inner Southerner. Since when do you say y'all?" Sam asked.

"First, it's *y'all* and not *yah awl*. It is a one-syllable word. Second, my friend from North Carolina taught me

how to use it, and it was appropriate in this situation."
Frances poked Sam's ribs.

"That's quite the rock. When did that happen?" Molly
asked.

"Now's the time. Guess the cat's out of the bag," Sam
said. "Everyone. We need to make sure y'all have a drink
in hand."

"Better but not quite right."

Frances stood perfectly still as she watched Sam run to
the cooler and grab several beers and pass them around.
In one smooth, quick hop she was up on top of the picnic
table. Frances took Sam's hand and joined her on top of
the table.

"We have an announcement," Sam said to everyone
gathered in a wide circle around the rooftop.

"I asked this beautiful woman to be my wife tonight.
And she said—"

Everyone erupted in a collective "Yes!" And a round
of "Cheers" reverberated through the gathered group of
smiling and clapping friends. Frances held up her hand
and showed off the ring. She turned to catch Molly
watching her. They shared a smile and Molly put her arm
around Emily.

"We have a wedding to plan!" Russell said.

"Did Russell just squeal?" Sam asked.

"Yes. Yes, he did because he loves planning weddings.
Not sure what you were planning but chuck it out the
window because you're getting a Russell wedding," Winter said, holding up her drink. "Cheers."

"I hadn't thought about the wedding," Frances said.
"We can't have people at the wedding, can we?"

"We can have our close friends," Sam said. "Maybe something like this?"

"What about a wedding at your favorite place on earth?" Russell asked.

"The museum?"

"Yes!" Russell let out another squeal of delight.

"The museum is closed. I don't know if they will be able to reopen and they have laid off so many of their staff. It is heartbreaking. The whole world is a mess."

"It is and that is why it is important to go forward and celebrate the life you have in the moment you have it," Dana said.

"Oh my god! Dana?" Frances ran over to her, stopping a few feet away. "Can I hug you?"

"Yes. And thanks for asking. Sam called me, which is why I had to get off the phone with you. She's been planning this for months. She was here in February buying your ring, you wingnut."

"Dana, you made me question—"

"You came to some answers, and I know they are right for you right now."

"Who knows what's going to happen," Molly said as she walked a little closer to Frances and Sam. "I'm so happy for you both."

Frances accepted Molly's hug. She felt a jolt of electricity from her touch and rested her head on Molly's shoulder.

"Frances, I will always love you," Molly whispered into her ear.

The words entered Frances's brain and traveled to every cell of her body. She was caught in Molly's undertow and knew that she needed to deal with this at the moment. Frances caught Emily watching the two of the them, and she stepped back out of the hug. "You are so important to me. Before you leave tonight, would you mind giving me some time? I need to share something with you."

"Yes. That can be arranged pretty easily. The boys are letting us stay in the guest loft. My house sold and the closing happened quickly."

"Is that the news?" Frances asked.

"Part of it. We can wait."

Frances turned from Molly and looked at Emily. Neither of them wore a ring. Frances felt it though. She knew that they had pledged themselves to one another. "Please share? There is more than enough love to share this evening. Everyone. Simon turn the music down—thanks."

The group gathered once again, and Winter and Cheryl both reached for a new beer. Sam walked over and took Frances's hand. Frances smiled and whispered a special word into Sam's ear and the two of them shared a smile.

Molly took her pocket knife out and rapped the side of her beer bottle to gather the attention of the group and then turned to Emily and took her hands in hers. "As you all know, Emily and I have taken things quite slowly. With everything going on and the police force giving me some much-needed time off, I went to visit Emily in Portland. I couldn't take it slow any longer. We are in love and we are going to marry. I don't want to waste any more time."

Frances was the first to shout congratulations. She hugged Emily first and then stood back as Molly was mobbed by the crew. This was truly exciting, and Frances took a huge breath and let out a sigh.

"That was a big sigh," Winter said. "She hasn't seen the paintings?"

"Nope. She told me that she would always love me."

"When? She did not. What the fuck? You lesbians confuse the shit out of me."

"This is a confusing world, but I know what she meant. She and Emily are so happy, and Sam and I are too."

"I know. You and Sam are stunning together, and I know you've had questions and those paintings downstairs are freakin' amazing. There is a light, an energy that you and Sam have when you're together that is spectacular."

"What's next?" Dana asked.

"Don't ask me. With our country going through a crisis of a pandemic and then a reckoning with its racial war—I hope we survive."

"We will survive—we've got two weddings! That is a gift," Russell said.

Frances turned to Sam and gave her a gentle kiss. "I love you and want to spend the rest of my life with you."

ALICE
"How long is forever?"

WHITE RABBIT
"Sometimes, just one second."

—FROM TIM BURTON'S FILM, ALICE IN
WONDERLAND

Sheila M. Sullivan lives in the Pacific Northwest with her wife and two Cardigan Welsh corgis. Before she started writing fiction full time, Sheila explored careers in stand-up comedy and then law. As an attorney, she practiced toaster-law—tackling whatever popped up through the office front door.

Sheila is the author of *Spectrum* and *Illumination*, books one and two in the *F.O.K. Series*, a cocktail of comedy, romance, and friendship served up with a twist of murder. Her novella *Pandemic Rabbits* follows the same characters as COVID-19 exploded around the world; book three in the series will be out in the fall of 2020. Her nonfiction book, *The Accidental Writing Lab*, shares how Sheila found her writing voice.